Mocha for Mateo

Also by Melanie Greene

Pier 3 Coffee Series

Mocha for Mateo *(Alicia & Mateo)*

Cappuccino for Callie *(Abraham & Callie)*

Latte for Leyla *(Austin & Leyla)*

Roll of the Dice Series

Rocket Man *(Serena & Dillon)*

Ready to Roll *(Janice & Miguel)*

Eye of the Tiger *(Natalie & Evan)*

Let the Good Times Roll *(Chloe & Gabriel)*

Roll of a Lifetime *(Rachel & Theo)*

Roll Play *(Kim-ly & Tómas)*

On a Roll *(Gillian & Vic)*

Roll in the Hay *(Anton & Cisco) - available to subscribers or as a bonus in the Roll of the Dice novella anthology*

Other Contemporary Romances

Retreat to Love *(Ashlyn & Caleb)*

Feather in Her Cap *(Jeannie & Brendan)*

Twelve Scorching Days *(Sarita & Scorch)*

Margo of the Bells (Margo & Karl)

Curiosity (Amity & Josh) - story in the It's Always Been You anthology

Mocha for Mateo

MELANIE GREENE

For information, contact Melanie Greene at mel@melaniegreene.com

First edition: June 2021

Mocha for Mateo/by Melanie Greene

ISBN: 978-1-941967-28-7

For all the Davids -

My dad,
who rocked everything about our intergenerational family
business
My son,
whose visions for the future inspire my fictional (and real)
worlds

Chapter One

Customers to Pier Three Coffee often walked in and pulled a dramatic, aroma-inhaling pose. Alicia's baristas called it the SuperBean Stance.

It wasn't that Alicia Wells didn't love the smell, too. She'd morphed into a coffee snob in college, and converted both her brothers while she was at it. Their shared addiction to a quality caffeine fix helped her brothers fall in with her plan to use their grandparents' inheritance to open a progressive independent coffee shop in their not-so-little-anymore town of Surfside. Just close enough to the Bay Area to enjoy the perks of Northern Californian life, and full enough of tourists and college students to funnel a steady stream of customers their way.

They'd succeeded, so far, in navigating more than their share of emotional and logistical obstacles. As long as they spent most of their waking hours working on it.

But she made sure, in the narrow slice of time between waking and working, to allow herself a moment to lean against the building and stare out towards the Pacific Ocean. Although it was past sunrise, the fog in front of her and the mountains behind her obscured the incoming tide. She didn't need to see the waves to be captured by them. She breathed in deep, savoring the salt air. A lesson she learned after her first few days living above the coffee shop: seize every chance to take in scents that weren't ground beans. All too soon, she would be enveloped by everything about Pier Three. Alicia loved the place, had spent three years fighting like a mythic boss for it, but she needed to keep a sliver of herself separate from the business.

And separate from her siblings. When they'd converted the old bait shop to a cafe, they'd also refurbished the apartment perched in its cupola. Her rent was low, with the trade-off that she was the partner to open up Pier Three Coffee each morning.

Always an early riser, it was no burden and it fulfilled her need for privacy. Abraham and Austin still shared a two-bedroom in the apartment complex their parents owned, up near campus. She'd been living above the cafe long enough now to almost sleepwalk through her opening routine: unlock the employee entrance, turn on the lights, check nothing had gone wrong overnight with the plumbing or fridges or anything, put the day's special blend in the grinder. Stretch and let the promise of her first macchiato bring her body alive.

Loiter in the doorway.

Meet the bakery van.

Check to see if Mateo was driving.

He didn't always. Mateo and his parents owned James Family Bakers, and sometimes events in their storefront meant he delegated the morning delivery run. Around seventy-four percent of the time—Alicia sometimes did math in her head for fun; it wasn't obsessive of her to know the statistic—Mateo was the one whose broad shoulders towered over the steering wheel as he nosed the van into the small parking area at the base of her staircase. Mateo's bare arms unlatching and hauling down the two-wheel dolly. Mateo's back flexing as he stacked up trays of scones and muffins and stuffed breads and paleo seed cakes, all ready to tempt the customers of Pier Three.

"Hey, A."

"M."

He did the thing with his cheek. The little flex hinting that he wasn't as laid back as his tone suggested. "Anyone else around?"

"Nope."

"Huh."

She waited. Not a hardship, the waiting. The van almost radiated yeasty warmth and sweet spices through the open doors. She drifted closer. "Busy morning?"

He shrugged. "Nothing unusual."

"Smells like a cardamom brioche day." Alicia leaned into the van to better capture the enticing odors that always evoked Mateo for her. In a regular van, the area would hold passenger seats, but for the bakery, a rack of deep shelves was bolted in where the third row of seats would be, and storage for the dolly and some supplies took the place of second-row seats. He slammed the van's rear door and wheeled the laden dolly through the shop's door. She followed.

In an effort to not ogle his ass while he unloaded his buns onto her shelves, she turned to start the day's first urn of drip coffee and update the specials board. He emerged from the kitchen as she stowed the whiteboard markers under the counter. "Got time for a coffee?"

Mateo shook his head. She felt ridiculous for noticing how his forearm flexed as he drew the dolly to a halt at the back door. But he extended that forearm her way, and the buzzing under her skin abated as they made contact. A few side-by-side steps, and she hitched herself into the van's interior while he slid the empty bakery trays into place.

She'd never set out to be so familiar with his routines. It felt habit-forming in the worst way. Too addictive and too every day and too centered on him instead of her. None of that was on her fuck-buddy checklist.

In the pro column, though, Mateo turned her on. Each of his movements, no matter that he was just doing his job, felt like a performance for her. The stretch of his muscles under his t-shirt, the silent-but-steady gauging of her pleasure, the way he flashed his eyes her direction while she arranged herself in his space. The direct, unambiguous way he approached her and gave her a look she could read no matter how diffuse the sun's early morning light in their enclosed corner of the world.

As she grabbed the overhead straps and pulled herself to her knees on the floor of the van, Mateo filled the inches between them so they were eye-to-eye, breath-to-breath. "Impatient today?"

She shrugged, as much as she could while half-dangling. "Weird dream about my grandmother. Thought I could clear the mental air with something more cheerful, you know?"

The man spent a great deal of time chopping ingredients, kneading and forming doughs, reaching into hot ovens with little regard for burns. Made zero sense, how he could smooth his much-abused fingers so soft over her brow and make her relax. He leaned into her, sent one hand skimming over the crown of her head and down her spine, so they ended up chest-to-chest.

She kissed him. He opened to her, tugging until they leaned together, his warmth as comfortable and welcome as that of the fresh-baked loaves beside them. Sometimes she wondered, away from these stolen dawn moments at the employee door, if his kisses, his touches, would enfold her the same way elsewhere. If they were in his apartment in the foothills. If she let him spend the night in her bed. If they came together anywhere besides his van, or the shadows of the parking lot, or quickly, when there was time, up in her room.

Enough ridiculous speculation. She dropped a hand down to his ass, stroked the familiar hard curve, and tucked her fingers under his waistband.

His cock responded, but he broke the kiss. "Can't today."

"Thought you weren't busy."

"Yeah, no." Mateo's hands were no more in agreement with this plan to skip morning sex than was the rest of his body. She arched as he palmed up the sides of her flannel shirt. They both groaned when her nipples tightened between them. His voice was as rough as his calloused palms. "Nothing unusual, except volume. Got to stick on schedule."

"Or be a few minutes late but ready to whistle while you work," she suggested, rocking her belly against his erection. She was balanced on the very edge of the van's threshold; if not for the blanket pad he always tossed right where she could rest on it, her knees would ache. But in his own not-talkative way, Mateo paid attention to things like that. Her comfort. Her needs. Her boundaries about how far he could intrude into her life.

Which—unfortunately for her libido—didn't put him at her beck and call. "No can do," he said, drawing back an inch that felt like a foot.

She dropped back to sitting. Reached for the sandals she'd slipped off during the kiss. "Well, damn."

"Damn indeed. Would so love to be fucking you right now."

She didn't need to say the feeling was mutual. He knew.

"I have something for you, though."

"Oh?" She glanced down, but his hand was only near his crotch so he could draw a baggie out of his front pocket. Alas.

"Not that."

"Spoil sport."

He snorted. "Spoiling my own fun, too, you know. Anyhow, here."

A light thud on the back of the van put them both on alert, turning outward.

"Hands off my sister, please," Abraham called from just out of sight.

She rolled her eyes but stepped clear of the van and smoothed down her shirt. It wasn't a secret that she and Mateo hooked up some mornings, and if her big brother couldn't deal with the idea of her having sex, that was his own issue. Still, she wasn't used to him showing up so early, and the irritation in her voice masked her concern. "What is your issue?"

Abraham nodded a greeting to Mateo, who stepped up behind her shoulder. She flashed with irritation that he was lurking close like she needed protection. When he bumped his crotch against her, she relaxed into the awareness that he wanted her to hide the bulge in his jeans.

"Good morning to you, too, sis."

"You don't even have a shift today."

"Thanks. I forgot how to read the schedule."

"Funny. Is something wrong?" Maybe her voice wavered some tiny amount, because Mateo ran a couple of fingers down her spine.

Abraham cleared his throat. "I'm giving you a heads-up so you can get ready. Mrs. Vallejo is stopping by in an hour."

She used to think, when they were little, that when she turned her eyes into fierce slits, they'd aim perfect laser darts at her unsuspecting and helpless brothers. It hadn't yet felled either of them, but Abraham did, at least, rock backwards.

"Why is Mrs. Vallejo coming by?" Mrs. V was their land-lady, and from day one of their negotiations, she'd done business via email. Abraham was the one who dealt with the lease, not that they didn't all have access if they needed it. Alicia's own interactions with her were enough to show that the woman was the least spontaneous person she'd ever met. "And when did she tell you about it?"

Abraham flushed some, the snake. "I'll fill you in over a coffee?"

"You sure as hell will. Did you tell Austin?"

He nodded. "He's on his way." And with that, he slithered his sneaky way into the shop, leaving her alone with a thousand questions.

And Mateo.

Broad palms cupped her shoulders, and she let herself sag. Let herself lean her back against his strong chest. Just for a minute, though. She had work to do.

Turning to face him, she flashed a perfectly calm smile. "Okay, good thing we couldn't have sex this morning after all."

Something not-best-pleased crossed his face, but she didn't have time to placate his ego.

She noticed the baggie tucked haphazardly next to his now-controlled bulge. She snagged it and shook it brisk and cheerful, to signal she was ready for him to head out. "What am I holding here?"

After a beat, he answered, "Cardamom, with a touch of cinnamon and ginger. Grated it when I was making the brioche this morning. Add a rounded half-teaspoon per cup for Israeli coffee. Thought you'd like it."

It smelled amazing. Distilled essence of his baking. The kind of thing to lift her spirits, to center her, if she found she needed such a thing from him. Alicia closed her hand around the resealed bag. "I'll add it to the specials, thanks."

Mateo's narrowed eyes were no good at making lasers. He lacked her killer instinct. "It's not for your customers, A. It's for you. If you want me to provide custom spice blends for your business, add them to the order form."

It would be juvenile to glare right back at him, and Alicia was not a juvenile. She was not as good at on-the-spot retorts as she'd like, but she was adult enough to let him be the one to end their stare-down.

He turned away to finish loading up the van, and much as she needed to dash upstairs for a shower and the uncomfortable armor of professional clothing, she waited. Standing there unable to think up a single good reply. Watching until he drove off into the brightening day without a word of farewell.

A half-mile up the beach road, Mateo pulled over to stare at the misty surf and calm the hell down. Hair-trigger temper but never a grudge, that was his reputation. Well enough earned, he'd admit, but not the whole story.

Seemed like no one ever wanted to get at the whole story.

The tide was on the way in, and he made out a couple of clumps of surfers, zipping into wet suits and idly chatting on the sand. They'd start their mornings on the waves, and like as not end up at Pier Three Coffee afterward, boards propped in the racks, gathered around picnic tables on the deck with coffee and his protein-rich baked goods, watching their fellows and fueling up for the day ahead.

And more power to them. He grabbed his tablet and updated the delivery to Pier Three, then double-checked his next stops. A few more deliveries, and it would be his lunch break. He could, as he sometimes did, swing back by Pier Three and let Alicia fix him a drink while he ate. But she would be stressing about the landlady, or snarking about his busy day, or subjecting him to her cordiality.

It wasn't secret, their ... relationship? Arrangement? He knew she was likely to classify it differently to him. Or she would be, if she ever did anything but evade both his hints and his direct questions, and be definitive. For months he'd taken her lead, and as a result, everyone knew they hooked up, but no one treated them like a couple. He could walk right up to her in the middle of Pier Three or out someplace with friends, and get a nod of hello. But never a hug, never a kiss. No one in the world could spy them in passing and guess they were more than friends. They'd have zero clue how he felt about her. And since she wasn't interested in hearing it from him, that left Mateo as his own secret-keeper.

Allowing himself another few seconds of Pacific breeze, he filled his lungs with enough ocean brine to temporarily stave off the omnipresent yeast-and-spice scents of the van.

Of his life.

He shifted into gear and went about his business. His family's business. Alicia sometimes talked like that gave them common ground, the family business thing. She never saw the differences. That she and her brothers were grown and through university before choosing to dovetail their career paths in order to work together. That they'd united with shared goals, and picked something that catered to their interests, combined their strengths, and allowed them to work towards a vision they built together. That they'd asked each other if the coffee shop was what they wanted.

He didn't begrudge them their unity. It wasn't part of his reputation, after all, to hold grudges. And Mateo, with really just the one exception, lived up to expectations. So Alicia had a tight-knit bond with her brothers. So they worked well towards mutually agreed upon goals. So they listened to each other.

Living without all that sucked a bit. But the tradeoff was, in being all that was expected of him as the 'Family' part of 'James Family Bakers,' he gave the extended family no room to react against the truth of the rest of him.

Chapter Two

"Want a scone?" Abraham asked.

Alicia waved him off. She was on the third page of notes after their meeting with Mrs. Vallejo, and wasn't going to let her brother interrupt her flow. He would be itching to launch into some kind of reframing or negotiation or rationalization and she was not in the mood.

"Tea?"

"Go away. We'll talk later."

"Lisha, come on."

"Go away, Abraham."

She didn't have to look up from her legal pad to know he was tilting his chin in that restrained-impatience way of his. Let him stew. Served him right for failing to mention the meeting until the last minute. She had schemes to concoct.

Their landlady's announcement that she wanted to sell the building wasn't a complete shock. She'd mentioned moving to Oregon to be closer to her grandkids back when they first signed the lease on the former bait shop they'd converted into a mostly thriving independent coffee shop. Alicia's long-term plans, from the outset, included buying Mrs. Vallejo out. But like a magical-thinking fool, she'd operated on the assumption they'd have until their five-year lease was up to build capital.

But then: recession, and Mrs. Vallejo losing her husband. It made total sense she'd want to sell to finance her move north, and their lease contract didn't give them much leverage. It was kind of Mrs. V to even offer them time to get financing before putting Pier Three's building on the commercial market. But realistically, no one buying out the remainder of their lease would turn around and sell it to Alicia and her brothers just two years later. Assuming the new owner even honored their lease.

"Lisha." It was Austin, clearly having been deputized by big brother to get her attention. She spared a moment while flipping over to a blank page to wave him off.

He didn't take the hint. Austin never took the hint if he didn't feel like it. He probably went out of his way to scrape the chair legs against the painted concrete floor as he seated himself across from her. Leaning up on his forearms, he made as if to read her notes upside down. "Whatcha writing?"

"Lists."

He drummed his hands on the table. "No shit. You probably have special markers so you can write lists on the tiles while you shower."

The quick cadence of his palms on the tabletop sent her pen jittering across the page, so she gripped it tighter and lifted the pad to rest on her left arm while she wrote. "You installed that tile; you know damn good and well there's no room to write on the mosaic."

"Abe says you fainted when Mrs. V said she's kicking us to the curb."

"I did not. And she's not kicking us out."

Only Austin could go from irritating her with his talking to goading her with his silence. She looked up, and he'd gone all soft and concerned. "We'll think of something. Don't worry, okay?" A gentleness in his tone screamed how ready he was to launch into overprotective mode.

On the one hand, it amused her when her irreverent little brother was so eager to copy Abraham's serious caretaker stance. On the collected other hands of everyone in the coffee shop—and that included Abe's prosthetic one—she had a perfectly functional older brother already. Austin should stay in his lane of backing off and letting his older siblings make the decisions.

He didn't let up even when she deployed her sternest big sister glare. She gave up first. "I'm not going to worry myself to death, okay? Just relax. Both of you."

Abraham grunted from where he'd paused behind her shoulder. After setting a hot, foamy chai at her elbow, he maneuvered to the seat beside her.

"You get freaked out about things like this."

She would never live down the rant about her old job that had led, more or less directly, to the three of them pooling their inheritance to found Pier Three. In no way did she regret that decision—their partnership meant an intense workload and all kinds of adjustments as they went from family to colleagues, but also a sense of power and liberation beyond her freest dreams. Still, she groaned each time one of her brothers alluded to her rant, and the circumstances that fed into it. Thank god she'd kept the other aspect of her workplace problems to herself, or they'd never let up.

"Dudes. Brainstorming is not the same as freaking out. I'm not on the verge of a panic attack. I'm just making those lists you like to hassle me about, not peeling the skin off your sunburnt noses."

Austin ducked his head to rub at the evidence he'd been surfing without sunscreen again. Abraham allowed himself a single syllable of laughter. "Drink your tea while it's warm."

She glanced at the spiced brew, flashing back to the baggie

of cardamom she'd stashed in her kitchen before dressing for the meeting. Pier Three's chai was her afternoon drink of choice, but just then she wasn't in the mood to tease her senses with anything intriguing and aromatic. She caught the barista's attention. "Ruthie, can you make me a tangerine soda, please?"

Unfazed, Austin reached across for the chai, which meant Abraham switched his surly gaze to their little brother. Good. The last thing she needed was the two of them teaming up against her before she had a chance to make her pitch for ways to finance buying the building. They were all equal partners. Most of the time, Austin left the decision-making to Alicia and Abraham. Not that he was a pushover by any means. When she and Abraham locked horns, he set himself up as the chilliest judge in Northern California, listening through their arguments and pushing back on both sides until the one he ruled against was ready to concede before he'd announced his verdict.

She could handle that. It was fair. What irked her was Austin siding with Abraham from the outset. It was no fun arguing with a couple of brick walls. And almost never effective.

"Okay, you've done your due diligence with the hovering and the monitoring my heart rate or whatever. Will you two give me credit for rolling with this punch now, so we can focus on what we do next?"

She didn't love the look that passed between her brothers. But Abraham leaned over to scan her notes, so she flipped to the first page and began to talk them through her initial ideas.

Mateo sent Sean out with the deliveries the rest of the week. All part of the new plan. The 'figure out if Alicia could love him, or was he trying to proof a relationship with expired yeast?' plan.

The first step was testing the quality of his own ingredients, as it were. Can't bake a prize-worthy loaf with weevil-infested flour. So in case he was doing what she thought, and conflating lust with love, he removed sex from the recipe. He had to get past the point of near-daily cravings for her touch, her smile, the curve of her neck. He'd not been forced to beat an addiction before, so he wasn't sure how long it would take.

For a few days, he argued with himself that it was long enough. He'd stayed away, and still found himself thinking about sharing a joke with her, or baking her favorite egg tarts, or worrying about the result of the landlady meeting. Everything that was connected to Alicia herself, not her ability to make him harder than his granite spice-grinding pestle.

In his more cynical moments, he knew it was his lust tempting him to take back the morning delivery. He wasn't lying to himself about missing Alicia, and worrying over her. Those were genuine emotions, and important ones. Ones that established the truth that his feelings went deeper than his basic attraction to her and what she could do with his erection.

But until that erection stopped dragging him to her like a divining rod, he focused on his new breakfast bread recipes and left the van keys in Sean's hands.

By Monday, he'd accomplished two things: perfecting an innovative mango-chili-lime muffin, and knowing that never talking to Alicia again was a worse fate than never touching her again. Armed with both, he made his way back to Pier Three.

She'd fit herself back into the full business attire she'd unearthed from the depths of her armoire, where she'd banished it in hopes of never needing it again. Ironed her shirt like it had a hope of shielding her vulnerable skin. Polished her pumps as if their gleam could distract the world from the way her ankles felt prone to wobbliness as soon as she put them on. Everything she did to prepare reminded her too well of those corporate days. Of being transparently trapped, surrounded by untenable dead ends.

Her well-organized portfolio was stashed in her car, ready for a run out to San Jose as soon as the bread was delivered and the morning barista arrived. No need to change her plans because Mateo deigned to show up, annoying her by pulling into the narrow space in a way she immediately knew was not Sean. He navigated not just with the precise aim born of many prior deliveries, but also with an easy curving turn that only a hard-up person would view as sexy.

Van parking was not a sexy activity.

She folded her arms against the cool morning breeze. When Mateo hopped out with his usual single-letter greeting, she just nodded in reply. He asked how she was; she shrugged to show she was fine though not overjoyed. He explained about his new products; she jotted notes to prove she understood their many desirable qualities.

It wasn't until the breads were shelved that he wedged his shoulder into the wall beside her. Practically cornering her. Yes, if she needed she could swing open the street door to escape. Didn't change the fact he was using his size to make himself present in her life. "Hey, A."

"Mateo."

"Miss me?"

She glared, because screw him and his teasing. "Sure, of course. Not having regular sex is too tragic."

He bit back his smirk, which was the wisest move he could

make other than just clearing out of her way. "We both know we miss the sex. That wasn't my question."

"Not this again. Look, I have a meeting to get to."

He tilted his head, but didn't otherwise shift his bulk. "Something to do with the landlady thing?"

"Timeline for buying this place just got urgent. We're trying for an SBA loan, but our banker here was cautious because of our first quarter reports. They've seen our seasonal shifts, and the general economic outlook. They know we're going to double our profits in the summer. So, I'm hoping being face-to-face with a lender will be persuasive, and I can make sure we've got everything they're looking for. I mean, I do according to the checklists, but how many times do these things come back with a request for something not on the list, you know?"

And like that, he'd gone from looming to almost embracing her. Providing a wall of warm muscle she could lean on, if only she nudged a fraction his way.

She waved a hand to sever the currents of connection. "Sorry, you don't care about any of that. It's our problem."

"I wouldn't say that."

"Of course it is. Abraham might be denying we can find the financing, but whatever happens, it's on him and Austin and me to figure it all out. And my plan will work. I think. It will."

"No one dares to doubt your plans."

Her dismissive hand slid, and not because she meant it to, up his forearm. It only happened because he loomed so close it short-circuited her nerve endings and she misjudged her personal space. She recovered fast, tucking her arms down at her sides and lifting her chin to show his nonsense didn't sway her. "My plans are solid, that's why it's going to work. I did the research and ran the numbers. CalFirst should have recognized that, but if they don't grasp the value of our business, we'll find someone who does."

"You tried FSCU?"

"They haven't called me back yet."

"I'll get Felipe over there to drop you a line. He carries our building and equipment loans."

A sizzle shot up her spine like the sharp hiss of the frother. She wasn't clear if she moved or if he did, but there was at last some breathing room between them. "No. Thanks anyway. I have things in hand with the lender in San Jose, and if it falls through, I can make my own contact with the business loans people at FSCU."

"He's a nice guy. Smart. If it gets you a meeting, why not let me call?"

"You don't need to give me your banker's bona fides, Mateo. I've already contacted them, which means I've already researched them and determined they'll meet our needs. I get that you're trying to be helpful, but like I said, there's no need. Thank you anyway. I've got this."

The rattle of the door handle beyond them meant Cleo had arrived for her shift. Alicia was free to go, so without waiting for Mateo to back his van out of her way, she hopped into her car and maneuvered onto the open road.

Chapter Three

Alicia's windows faced the Pacific. People clamored for views like hers, full of scuttling clouds and waves crashing over the nearby rocky tide pools, a cycling rotation of sea birds, surfers and sailors and sea mammals moving past.

Plus, the sunsets. So many gorgeous sunsets, blues and oranges and pinks and yellows and this one dark lavender shade of purple she'd come to think of as the universe's personal gift to her soul.

In a dark lavender kind of mood, she turned on some Joni Mitchell and stepped onto her balcony to watch the sun dip behind a cloud bank. Twilight was meandering in, and she had every intention of positioning herself around the bonfire before anyone else in their group could show up to claim her favorite spot. As much as she loved Pier Three, she always wanted to sit with her back to it during their Friday evening bonfire meet-ups. She wanted to fill her horizon with the ocean and the lights of town blinkering up into the mountains behind it. Just to give herself an hour or two when she wasn't focused on work or home either one.

She spotted her cousin Noah parallel parking a ways up

the beach. And a couple of friends from the university leant against their hatchback, trading work shoes for flip flops. She finished toweling off her hair and moved inside to grab a serape and the six-pack chilling in her fridge. No guitar this night; she wasn't in a strumming kind of mood. Noah met her at the edge of the fire pit and helped her spread out the blanket, anchoring one corner with the beer before claiming a spot for himself.

As she settled, she asked, "So, what's up with Surf Fest?"

Noah grimaced and slumped dramatically against her. "Oh my god, don't even go there. Do you know how many council member biographies I've memorized over the past week? Just to figure out a way to negotiate one measly permit."

"It's not looking good?"

He snorted. "I had no idea this town was such an old dude's club. Or old gal's club if you count how nothing's gonna get done if Astrid Plunkett doesn't think you're worthy."

"Why doesn't Astrid Plunkett think you're worthy?" asked Austin, taking up residence on the other side of the blanket.

Alicia bumped her shoulder into his, partly as welcome and partly in gratitude that now Mateo would have to look for someplace else to sit. She left Noah and her brother to discuss the Plunkett problem while she scooted forward to build a proper fire out of the wood her friends had dropped by the pit. Just as she was coaxing the kindling into a flame, she felt eyes on her.

She glanced up and: yep. There was Mateo, arms crossed like the skeptic he was.

"What?" she asked.

"You're never going to build the logs into a tent shape, are you?"

She rolled her eyes at him and went back to tending the flames. "Log cabin works great," she said, once she wedged herself back between her relatives.

He shook his head. "It's not a fireplace, A. Haven't you ever seen a child's drawing of a campfire? It's a triangle for a reason."

"Can't you two ever give it a rest?" Abraham asked, making his way over. He nudged Austin. "Make way."

Austin leaned back on his elbows like the thought of moving had never occurred to him. "Bring your own blanket if it's so important to you."

She shot eye-lasers at them. "I'm the one who brought the blanket." Her brothers ignored her.

Across the pit, Mateo unstuffed his nylon mat and shook it out. "I've got room."

Austin poked her with his foot. "Go sit with Mateo so Abraham can sit down."

"It's my blanket," she repeated.

Noah handed Austin one of her beers, then pointed his own in warning. "Careful, she's got her boss bitch voice on."

"Must be left over from the other day." Mateo gave Abraham a hand to sit down beside him.

"Why, what happened the other day?" Noah asked.

It was plenty light enough for her to catch the way Mateo glanced at her before he answered Noah. Like he wanted to be sure he hadn't cast any of her secrets out to the waves. Whatever her face was like, it gave him some kind of leave to continue. "She was all kitted out in a suit to go to meetings. It was fierce. Powerful."

Suddenly everyone was talking around her like she wasn't on the beach. She leaned forward to prod at her bonfire, which was sparking up very nicely, thank you very much. Austin finished explaining about the quest for bank loans and Mateo put in, "The main thing is she looked like a total boss.

You know how sometimes she gets that determined face? And you're like, I sure hope the baristas don't mess up that customer's order."

Noah laughed. "When we were kids, I told Uncle Simon that his daughter scared me. And he told me he'd give me five bucks if I would tell her that to her face."

Everyone was laughing, but she glared.

"Yes, just like that," Noah said, pointing.

"Did you do it?" Austin asked, leaning against her like she wasn't scary at all.

"God no."

Mateo turned to Abraham. "You suppose your dad would still make that deal?"

Austin snorted and answered for them all. "I doubt he'd think he could find any takers at this point. God knows Dad loves when people are intimidated by his daughter."

"Seems like he and I have something in common, then," Mateo said, all attention locked on her. "Alicia being intimidating is one of those things that I can't get enough of."

Suddenly, it wasn't possible to look away from her sometime lover. He was smoldering more than the damn slow-to-catch outer logs on her fire.

Noah chucked a bottle cap his way. "Every damn thing about Alicia is something you can't get enough of. Don't play like you're not soft on her."

Mateo took the cap and tucked it into his recycling tote. "Who says I'm playing?" He asked it so quietly that if the smoke between them had drifted even a little bit his way, she wouldn't have been able to read the message on his lips.

Noah and Austin had helped her finish off her beers, so she slumped back against the serape, letting her eyes adjust to the darkness above. Alicia wasn't sure why she stood for the bonfire gang teasing her about Mateo. It wasn't really any of their business if the two of them got together sometimes.

They were a close-knit bunch, getting closer over the years as they established the routine of weekly beach bonfire nights for anyone with the time and inclination. Pretty much all of them worked mornings—few as extremely early as Mateo's bakery job, but plenty of them were at their jobs before the tourists and students in Surfside groaned about their morning alarms. Their energy faded as the sun set over the Pacific, so their version of nightlife involved chatting and drinking on the beach before heading early to bed.

She loved how bonfire nights anchored her to the town and her community. She'd clung to those anchors in the years they'd been establishing Pier Three, and then even more while busting ass to keep it afloat during the recession.

The closer she felt to the bonfire group, though, the more she was exposed to the kind of banter she'd merely witnessed, back before she and Mateo sparked with each other one Friday. They'd cuddled some before that week, while she steadfastly ignored the occasional incursion of his lips on her nape or the top of her head. But that bonfire night, for whatever reason, she'd kissed his cheek in return, and they'd spent the next three days in bed.

She didn't balk at anyone knowing about her fuck buddy. But combined with the newness of Mateo's intense and public praise, the jokes set her insides to squirming.

And not in the good way she was used to when he was around.

She wasn't at all sure she liked it.

Did she think she wasn't transparent to him? Hard to imagine how she could feel that way, given how every nascent thought flicked across her face. So, it wasn't exactly a shock when she sat up and shoved her brother's head off her shoulder.

"Hey."

"Hey yourself," she grumped right back. "I'm turning in."

"Fine. Good night."

"And that means you need to get off my blanket."

Austin nestled further into the sand. Her cousin followed suit.

"You two are useless."

"You're the one who complains that we're always leaving you the job of bringing stuff down here and cleaning it up afterward. Seems like a more equitable division of labor if you go away and leave us alone. I'll bring the serape by when I come in for my next shift."

"Yeah, and is it going to be crusted over with sand and beer stains?"

"No, because I am a thoughtful and responsible human being."

Beside him, Abraham coughed, "Bullshit."

Their brotherly bickering made a decent distraction from Mateo's rising to follow Alicia, who was heading off with nothing more than a pointed look at Austin and a wave to everyone else. As he stood, Abraham tapped him on the shin. He looked down to the man's outstretched hand. Wordlessly, he dropped the carry bag for his sand blanket in his lap. Abraham nodded even while continuing to give his brother shit, which suited Mateo plenty. He didn't know if Alicia would even let him catch up to her, much less join her in her apartment. But he appreciated the quiet indication that his friend would look out for his stuff if he didn't make it back soon.

Once he was clear of the firelight, he jogged to catch up to Alicia. She was walking fast, arms folded tightly in a way that read to him as defensive rather than chilled.

He wasn't oblivious. He knew damn well that she'd just as soon no one mentioned how he looked at her. Thing was, unless she told him straight out otherwise, no way was he going to stop looking. That being the case, the gang was going to notice. And the gang being the gang, they were going to comment, especially her wiseass cousin.

"Alicia." The wind was the wrong way, but obviously, his voice carried enough for her to notice.

She slowed and dropped her arms, though she didn't turn or wait for him.

He caught up a few feet short of the Pier Three patio. "Hey." And then his mind blanked. Whatever instinct had pushed him to follow her into the night, hadn't been so kind as to let him know what to say once he got to her.

Alicia didn't have the same problem. "I hate those business suits."

"Okay?"

The question in his voice prompted her to go on. "When I left Zenon, I had a whole closet of them. More than a closet. That armoire in my place now? That's where I kept all the overflow, whatever wouldn't fit into my walk-in. Some of it was external pressure, you know? Everyone else looking the part and me feeling like I needed to match." Her lips pressed together in a way even more defensive than her crossed arms had been.

"And the rest of it?" He'd never pegged her as an especially vain or status-obsessed person. But he hadn't known her in her corporate businesswoman days.

"The other part was ..." She sighed and leaned up against the patio rail. "It was a kind of costume. I thought if I could put on the right kind of clothes, I would fit the profile."

Obviously, his few accounting classes and the small business conferences he'd attended hadn't been much use at cluing him in to the pressures she'd been facing. "You wanted to fit this profile and felt like you didn't?"

She shrugged in a way that left her leaning lightly against

him. He couldn't figure how deliberate a movement it had been, but he'd take it.

"Sometimes it was more a case of trying to convince myself that I did fit in. I'd done all that work to get the damn job in the first place. And even when it—well, when what happened, happened, I knew I had to find someplace new." She bit her lip and he swallowed down his barrage of questions about what had sent her away from her high-power job in corporate hospitality. It was something she never brought up. And he knew from her body language she was in no mood to get explicit about it now.

"I interviewed other places, even got a couple of offers. One was where a friend of mine from grad school worked, so I knew all about the corporate culture there. Knew I wasn't going to end up in the same ..." She shrugged again. "Anyhow. Point is, I had the chance to stick with it. To find a use for all those suits."

"But instead you ended up here."

She nodded.

"And you don't want to revert to a place where you have a closet full of costumes. Even though, far as I can see, you more than earned the ability to fit in wherever you want."

"It doesn't matter if I fit in. It matters that I don't want to. That's not who I want to be."

Ah. He nodded. "So when I called you out for being a badass boss bitch, you didn't want to hear how impressive you were to me, or how I admire your knowledge and capabilities. You just heard that I was hot for some superficial dress-up version of you, and that sent you scrambling."

He immediately paid the price for daring to have any insight into her heart. Alicia was halfway to her staircase before he'd even stood up. He followed just close enough to hear her lock herself in her apartment before turning to follow the beacon of the bonfire back to his circle of friends.

Chapter Four

Everything was asphalt and gas fumes and he couldn't breathe in even a hint of ocean from the scorching midday air. He called the bakery to let them know the van had overheated behind an accident that had traffic snarled up through town. A passing cyclist helped him navigate to the curb and out of danger, and in return Mateo gave him a box of potato rolls. The guy asked for his number to go along with the bread, tipping his chin up with laughter when Mateo slapped a hand against the bakery's contact info on the side of the van.

The look in his eye might have burned and intrigued on another day. A day when Alicia hadn't—yet again—frozen his skin with her icy insistence on keeping their sex life sealed off from everything else that kept her alive. Sometimes she'd share her joys, but never her sorrows. Only inadvertently her troubles. Wayward wisps of her dreams. Not one piece of her past.

Before they'd slept together, he thought he belonged in the inner chambers of her heart. Sitting around beach bonfires with her and her brothers and the rest of their early-to-bed gang, watching the sunset, tossing sticks at the flames, and bullshitting about their lives. Overblown stories with confessional truths embedded inside. Unexplored sparks when limbs slid together in passing. Friendly kisses turned intentional when they had the screen of too much alcohol to blame.

And then she went home with him. No excuses, no pretenses. She led him to his own bedroom, deliberate. And stayed for three days, despite his rising before four every morning. He'd spent those days whistling while he worked, no matter how often his dad repeated, "Settle down, Matt."

Settle down.

Easier said than done. After the initial rush of exploring each other inside out, Alicia retreated to Pier Three and established the routine of morning delivery sex. No more sleeping over, no stopping by after work. Sitting away from him at bonfires. Never hiding that they slept together, never suggesting they stop. Rolling her eyes when he hinted at romance.

Someone honked and he swiveled to glare. Nothing he could do about the van until it cooled down, and nothing was cooling down anywhere around him just then. The day was too long as it was, and he had one last delivery to make before turning in the keys for good. Sean could drive every run in the future. He didn't have to keep searching for respite in Alicia's arms. She didn't want his heart or soul, and plenty of people—the biker who'd waved with elaborate sass as he pedaled off was just one example—would be happy to keep him around for his body.

The irritated driver edged past. The sun baked the air around him, and half an hour dripped by before the van cooled. When he finally got it back to the bakery, his father met his announcement about no more driving with, "Settle down, Matt."

Two mornings later, Sean did not show up. No call, no text, no astral projection to tell them where the hell he was.

Mateo tried to palm the deliveries off on someone else, but

his father just said, "Don't make everything so complicated, Matt." His mother gave him her, 'Do you want your papi's blood pressure to go haywire again?' look. So he grabbed the keys.

Pulling into Pier Three, he thought that for once Alicia was not waiting for him. That idea flew out the window when she clattered down the stairs from her apartment. Each thud on the metal treads as she descended reverberated in him. Right as he stepped out and shoved the door closed, she came to a halt. Five steps up but he caught the brief flare of her eyes and flush of her cheeks.

"A."

She took it as an invitation. His syllable still hung in the air, and she'd bounced down to the concrete and right up against him. Her hands on his ass, her teeth grazing his ear. Undulating. And maybe he meant to brush her off. Maybe his intentions could have held. It was possible she could be put off, despite his breath hitching. Despite his hardening cock. Despite the way his heart raced at the proof that she's missed at least one part of him.

Then she moaned and murmured, "Please come upstairs," and his resolve dissolved like sugar in warm milk.

She'd gone too long without touching the man. Not so long that she'd forgotten about his whole arrogant 'Don't you just pine for me when I stay away? Don't I know you better than you know yourself?' line of questions.

Just long enough for her to throw out any notion of playing like she didn't want him.

Seemed she was in luck. No protests about deliveries, no badgering her to proclaim some goddamn undying love. Just their bodies, their mouths, their heat.

Exactly what she wanted. All the physical fun with none of the forcing of emotional nonsense. A fabulous stress reliever, a hit of energy to start her morning, a respite from all the goddamn thinking she always had to do.

She tugged him by the wrist, backing them into her apartment. He was still in his baking clogs, and she ignored that she knew what it meant that he'd left his sneakers at home. He hadn't intended to deliver that day. Which meant this was not a planned fuck.

Didn't mean she couldn't enjoy it. Didn't mean her heart wasn't racing or her clit wasn't thrumming with each move they made together. Part of the sex buddies compact—pretty much all of the sex buddies compact, in fact—was orgasms whenever they were both free, and no need to make any elaborate date-like plans first. Less romance, more thrusting.

Her bed wasn't more than thirty steps from the door, even with navigating her folding screen and ottoman. Barely enough time to kick off her sandals and strip off her shift dress, but she managed. Mateo, the show-off, contrived to be balls-out naked in the same span. Alicia wasn't going to let him win, so her undergarments were on the floor when she scooted across the bed to open her bedside table. And then it was a tussle between them: tongues, condom, legs, nipples, hips, rolling and pinning and opening and moaning.

"Fuck, you smell good."

"You're the one who's all yeast and sugar."

He nudged his nose along her collarbone. "I smell like work. You smell like you. Hot and salt and coffee."

"That's the beach and work." She laughed because: fun. She and Mateo were only about fun.

Growling, he bit at her shoulder and thrust deep and fast into her. It stopped her breath for longer than felt possible. She was poised and edgy. His hand shackling her wrists was the only anchor stopping her free-fall. She felt almost shy when she raised her gaze to meet his.

"When you laugh, I feel it to my toes," he said.

Just that, all soft and intent and low. Serious. And then his lips brushed her nipple, and she gasped in all the air she'd been missing, and he pivoted his hips that way he had whenever they made it to a horizontal surface, and she plummeted into orgasm.

Chapter Five

His chest hadn't caught up to his breath yet, but she swatted at his shoulder. "Time to get back to work."

"Huh."

"I mean it. I have reports to run."

"Everything worked out with the bank?" He didn't know why he bothered asking. One syllable of friendly concern and she bounded off the bed, leaving him cold in the morning air.

"It's all good, or it will be."

He scrubbed at his scalp as he sat up. Sniffed his pits. Five deliveries left, followed by four more hours at the bakery. "I'm hopping in the shower."

She unearthed her robe from the pile of clothes on her ottoman. "Suit yourself."

Her bathroom was tidy for once. Nothing overflowing the hamper; clean towels stacked in the rack. Those first days she'd spent at his place, he'd offered to pick up any kind of product she liked, and was met with derision. "Why can't my hair get just as clean as yours with your shampoo?"

Which, fine, was a point. And it wasn't that he expected her to be high maintenance because of her gender; he'd been with men whose toiletry budgets were triple his. In truth, he'd offered because once he started spinning dream-webs about her being in his place all the time, he wanted to shore up those dreams by making his space comfortable for her.

Maybe that over-eagerness had spurred Alicia shutting down his romantic side. Maybe he'd been such a sap she thought he was a sure bet on her terms. Maybe he rolled her way every time she refused to meet him in the middle.

Hanging up his towel and slipping back into the clothes that hadn't been all the fresh at four that morning, he contemplated, again, some more, his next moves. When he emerged from the bathroom, she was tucked up in her computer chair, not glancing his way.

"Shop unlocked?"

Nothing like the reluctant half-tilt of her head to convey the monitor was of far more interest than his words. "Sorry?"

"For the delivery. Is the door unlocked?"

She shook her head slow, then fast and decisive as she stood and approached. His keys and hers were entangled in a straw bowl on the hall table; she made short work of separating them and tossing his at him as she held the door for them to head down.

At the base of the staircase he paused, looking out across the parking area towards the pier and the Pacific beyond. High tide, and no fog for once.

"You unloading, or what?"

Mateo turned her way. She'd pulled on shorts and a tank under her robe, and knotted her dark hair up in a bun. "It's a pretty morning, come see."

He watched her weigh the path of least resistance before walking the few feet between them. He took her hand and wove them past the parking signs until they stood at the edge of the beach. A few people fished off the downside of the pier, and the surfers kept the truce by staying on the northernmost waves. The sun was low enough that the water was mostly dark, with purple-pink hints as it lapped the shore.

"Nice." She squeezed his hand as she said it; he was hyper-alert to her pulling it away, but no. She rested against his side as the breeze skimmed along their skin.

"Mmm." He agreed. He lifted his phone with his spare hand. "Selfie?"

At that, she straightened. "Not before my first cup of coffee."

"I didn't wake you up plenty? Cause we can go again."

"Ha." She retreated towards the cafe.

"Fine." He put his back to the ocean and aimed the camera. By the time he was satisfied with his shot, she was waiting inside Pier Three for him.

Not another word from her as he worked. She leaned against the strip of wall between the bathroom and supply closet doors, watching him. Looking away when he caught her eye. Sitting in the silence that descended after the clunk and rattle of the dolly he wheeled over the threshold, nothing but the wind-rushed waves echoing the watery feeling in his gut.

She would never bend to his will, which was amazing and beautiful to him. Her self-possession and determination and surety. If ever there was a person no one would snap at to get it together and be decisive, it was Alicia. Sometimes he didn't know if he admired her or wanted to body-swap with her.

Regardless, he'd learned a few lessons by observing her tight control in the months they'd been hooking up. So far, neither those lessons, or his own instincts, had prompted the changes he so deeply desired. It was time for a new tactic, even if he broke his own heart deploying it.

He took a steadying breath, braced his feet to ground himself, and faced her.

Their little stroll meant her feet were itchy with sand, and the sex meant she needed a shower, and her deadline for the loan officer meant her spreadsheets were calling. So he didn't need to act so life-and-death about her little impatient gesture when he pulled out his phone again.

"What do you think?"

The wet sand was a drying crust between her toes. She barely glanced at his screen. "Of?"

"This pic."

Oh, it was reassure the handsome man time, was it? "You know you're a hunk. It looks great."

"The chef coat isn't too weird with the ocean background?"

She looked again. She'd not noticed his work clothes, really. Mostly it was just his eyes and the locks of breeze-ruffled hair and the way the morning light limned the sharp line of his jaw. "I mean, that's just what you look like. Are you putting this on Instagram or something? Hashtag morning break while the waves break?"

He snorted a light laugh. "No. I thought I'd use it for my profile pic."

"What about the plan to be the last man in California not on Twitter?"

"It's not a plan, I don't have a stance about it. It just gets too binary when I look for my place there, so I skip it. Besides, I meant my dating profile."

There was sand grit on her calves, too. She wanted to rub it off but he'd probably read it as her being uncomfortable or something. And she only cleared her throat because the salt air choked her up a little. "You're on the apps?"

"Well, not yet. No." He stashed the phone in his pocket, like he wasn't willing to share the glow of his image with her anymore. "But I want a dating life, A. What we have ..."

"The sex."

An upward nod. "Yes. The sex. It's great. And I'd rather date you than anyone else I know. But since you won't, and I need more, I've got to meet people. Online seems like a good place to start."

Sand, or salt, or maybe the dawn was breaking enough to awaken whatever little bugs slept overnight and couldn't wait to start biting at her limbs in the morning. Something made her itch. "You're going to date people and fuck me?"

"If I get to that point with someone else,"—he didn't drop his gaze"—we're done. Or if it bothers you, we can stop now."

Her breath was steady. Or no less steady than usual after they'd been together. "Why would I be bothered?"

"No. You wouldn't. Of course." He ran a palm over his hair. "So. I'll just let you know."

"Or keep your pants zipped next time you deliver, that'll be our sign."

Mateo nodded. Short and flat-eyed. She didn't feel like smoothing over his mood. She had hydrocortisone to locate and quarterly reports to run. She didn't so much as squeeze his ass as he hefted the empty dolly into the van.

One thing she had to check, though, before he left. He was strapping in the dolly, so she spoke to his broad back. "You aren't—you wouldn't date my cousins?" Noah and Valerie had both been known to go all giggly making innuendos about him, and she didn't want to watch how they would preen and press against his sturdy strength.

Mateo turned. If he'd batted an eye, she'd missed it. "No, A. You're the only Wells I want to fuck."

She retreated upstairs before he could slam himself into the front seat and take off for his next destination.

Chapter Six

The guy—Jaxson—from the afternoon of the overheated van
came into the shop. Mateo might not have clocked him, except
for the way he kept bouncing up on the balls of his feet to peer
beyond the register counter. He'd been standing at the pass-
through bundling receipts, and Jaxson's treetop height and
fuchsia beanie caught his attention.

The guy's eyes quirked up happily when he rounded the
corner. "Hey, bakery man. I wasn't sure I'd find you here."

In the grip of habit, he scrubbed his hands with the tail of
his apron before extending one for a shake. "Mateo James.
Nice to see you again."

"Oh, part of the famous James family? Maybe I didn't
have to worry you'd be fired for failing to deliver on time."

The cheesy, flirty reply about always delivering on time
froze on his tongue. He wasn't expecting to fall into banter
like that. Swallowing back the words, he went for an expansive
gesture with his arms. "Job security and all the buns I can
eat."

So much for not flirting.

Jaxson introduced himself, fumbling with the strap of his

backpack in an objectively cute way. Mateo tipped his chin towards an open table. "Got time for chat?"

"If you've got time, I've got time." He held up a bakery bag full of cookies. "Probably you've had your fill, but I'm willing to share."

"Give me just a sec."

And like that, his apron was on a hook and he was on a date. Or something that disoriented him like a date. Something any onlooker would code as a date. Chatting, asking get-to-know-you questions, eye contact.

Exchanging numbers.

Jaxson asked, and what was he supposed to do, suggest that the man show up and buy cookies anytime he wanted to talk to him? Rude. Besides, he dropped hints about going up to Pride together. It made him feel craven, but bitter experience taught him that turning up with men let him relax into automatic inclusion in ways he didn't get if his date's gender was female. Sometimes he just wanted to dance without being side-eyed as an interloper.

Bi-erasure: everyone's doing it. Sometimes he even did it to himself.

And, yeah, he'd figured out it was self-defensive, to erase a part of his identity before Papi could. Didn't mean he wasn't suppressing some temper at himself.

The real problem, as always in the past months, was that all else being equal, Alicia was the person he wanted to be with. Cute young draftsmen with a hankering for his ginger-snaps were great for his ego, but his heart was still bruised. She hadn't sent word or stopped by in the nine days since he'd been clear that he wanted more. No sunset knocks on his door, no cryptic messages on the cafe order forms, no texts. As far as he could tell, she'd forgotten he existed. So, his more-fragile-than-expected ego was very much out of sorts.

From the register counter, Eleanor sent him a matronly

wink of approval as Jaxson left. He headed back to his receipts, sticking in his earbuds so he could pretend to not overhear anyone's gossip about him. He'd spent a week ignoring sympathy about his broken heart, hints about young people he should meet, snark about Pier Three. He'd only broken his calm facade one, when Sean was nasty about Alicia, only to find him and the other bakery guys watching with smirks that showed he'd been goaded into the outsized reaction.

Hair-trigger temper but never a grudge, he'd reminded himself, and let it go.

A hand clamped on his shoulder and his dad, louder than necessary despite his playlist. "Matt."

He startled and turned, searching his father's face for signs of redness or strain. "Papi, what's wrong?"

"Calm yourself, Matt. Always jumping, and never in any direction but to the wrong conclusions."

Right, because there was not the least cause for concern. His dad's latest checkup had ended in a detailed lecture about lifestyle modifications, and his mom was in Sacramento at the moment, visiting Tia Alma. Mateo had the cardiologist's number in his favorites and never left the bakery unless Eleanor was on shift. Her CPR training was out of date, but it was better than nothing.

"Okay, I'm calm," he lied. The argument wasn't worth raising Papi's blood pressure. "Did you need anything?"

"Just the name of that equipment rental place."

Mateo glanced through the door to the kitchens. "Something broke down?"

His dad shook his head. "Ticking along great here. Stop fretting."

"Right. Good." He pulled out his phone and started scrolling through contacts.

"Hustle up, son. I've got Abraham Wells tying up the phone line in there, looking for help. Something with their refrigeration. Need to give him the info so I can call your mom back."

Oh, not acceptable. Mateo headed to the office, ignoring the admonitions of his apparently still-healthy dad.

He picked up the receiver. "Abe? What's up?"

"Mateo. Hey, it's the big fridge. Alicia thought it was just dirty fan blades, but the thermostat's not right and I'm worried about the coils. Repair can't get out here for a couple of days, so I thought I'd check with that equipment rental place you mentioned."

He was patting his pockets for keys and double-checking Eleanor was on shift until closing while Abraham rambled on. "I'll grab my tools and be right over."

"No, man, I can't ask—"

"You didn't ask. See you in five." He hung up, texted his sister about his leaving Papi on his own, and told his lurking dad, "Phone's all yours. I'll bring dinner by later."

Ignoring Papi's inevitable protests about not needing to be babysat, Mateo headed out to do battle with a refrigerator and, if he had his guess, a very irritated Alicia.

She'd shoved the shelving unit as much out of the way as it got, and moved the desk chair and a couple of bags of whole beans out to the delivery door's parking area. Wedged into the space she'd created, she shone her flashlight under the unit in search of any leaks or cracks or invading imps she could sweep away and have just this one problem of her life be easy to solve.

Someone came in and thunked something heavy and rattly down on the concrete floor before nudging her tennis shoe. She twisted out of the space and swept back the hair that had fallen from her messy bun. Mateo stood there looking like the patron saint of handymen, with one hand on the side of the unit as if to confirm that it was, indeed, not chilling anything.

Her own temperature was climbing higher. She started to ask what the hell he was doing, but Abraham answered that question by stopping in the doorway and clapping his hand on Mateo's shoulder.

"Thanks for coming, man. You didn't need to do that."

Mateo shrugged. "We have one of these 1200 series, too. There's a thing with," he waved his hand in a half circle like that made any sense, "it set us back a bit last year, but I took notes on how to reset it. It's not tricky, just one of those things they don't put in the owner's manual so you end up paying for repairs or upgrades instead of getting the chance to maintain it yourself."

He reached down. Did he think she needed help to rise from her awkward position? She had one leg stretched into the limited floor space, the other curled under her so she could use it to leverage herself behind the fridge. She'd pretzeled herself into this mess. She could get herself out.

Mateo didn't take her glare for an answer though, just leaned further towards her and liberated the flashlight she was holding. "It should be behind this panel." He shone the light on the other side of the unit, barely glancing to see she'd cleared out of the way before shoving a hulking mass of broken machinery into the place she'd just occupied.

She couldn't get past him to see what he was looking at, but just like that he'd boxed her in. He tilted into the newly created space and ran the light down the back corner of the unit. "Yeah, here it is. I'm not positive this will do it, but hey."

He handed Abe the flashlight and crouched to dig in his toolbox before straightening. He briefly met her eyes. "I gave Abraham the number of the equipment rental place in San Jose, on the chance this doesn't do it. And I loaded a couple of coolers into my car in case you need us to store anything at the bakery while you wait. He said you already checked the fan? And I'm guessing you didn't find any leaks down there."

He had to go and acknowledge her work, plus ensure she knew he was responding to a request for help, instead of charging in and taking over like she had no independent skills. For days and days now, she'd been wondering if he would come back to restart their arrangement. And instead of pestering her or yelling about his poor deprived prick, he was going out of his way to be respectful and friendly and helpful without stepping over any boundaries. Not asking anything of her heart.

Looking like a goddamn snack while doing it, too.

She wiped her overheated face on her sleeve.

When he paused to check for some kind of miracle refrigerator repair solution on his phone, she shot the glare of aggravation he so richly deserved Abraham's way. She could shove past Mateo, and her brother, too. Leave them to it. Or stay trapped in the corner of the office with nothing to do but watch Mateo's muscles flex and shift as he worked on her broken unit.

She wasn't in the mood to risk touching Mateo to get by, so she leaned back against the filing cabinet and pointedly did not stare at his thigh.

Because, fine, he was taking time out of his work day when they had an equipment crisis.

Fine, he had expertise he was sharing like the refrigerator whisperer of Surfside.

Fine, the laughing triumph in his voice when his trick worked, and the refrigerator churned back to life, appealed on some gut-twisting level.

Fine, he offered Abraham a double high five in celebration of the repair, when she knew it pissed her brother off that way too many people treated his prosthetic like it was untouchable.

Fine, fine, fine, fine. *Fine.*

She took her flashlight and slammed it back into the desk drawer. Shouldered the shelving and refrigerator back into place. Abraham gave her a slight shake of the head and finally cleared out of the office doorway.

She crossed her arms at Mateo. He'd saved them not just the expense of the repair, or, worse, a replacement, but the time lost and the food that would have gone bad. "Thanks for that."

He smirked at her petulant tone. Swept her a bow. "Glad I could be a service."

Since the alternative was to slam him against the humming fridge and plaster her mouth to his, she stomped away and up her stairs for a too desperately needed cool shower.

Chapter Seven

She was almost ready to head down to the bonfire when Austin rap-tapped her door.

"What's up?"

He thumbed over his shoulder. "Thought I'd say as how I readied a couple of thermoses of spiked coffee today."

"Nice. Did you need to grab some go-cups?"

He scowled at her. "No, I got cups and everything ready to take down to the beach. I just figured you might want to skip the beer tonight, since I took care of drinks."

"Right." She shouldered her guitar and scooped the rolled serape blanket from the basket next to her cane tree. "You need help carrying it over?"

"No." Austin crossed his arms. "I don't need anything. I just stopped to tell you what I had, not to get treated like a kid who doesn't understand how to pack a tote bag."

How did he always launch head-first into such defensiveness? She raised a placating hand. "Great, thank you, you're the best. Is it decaf, or what?"

"Two thermoses of decaf, one of regular, that Sumatran medium roast."

"A pleasure for every palate."

"Exactly. So are you ready to go, or what?"

She shoved his shoulder to push him out the door and let it click shut behind them. "Absolutely, little bro." And because every once in a while she fit the stereotype of a peacemaking middle child, she tousled his hair as she followed him down the steps. "Thanks for making the coffee. It's a great idea for bonfire nights. If we do it again, we should ask Mateo to bring some of that biscotti they make."

Maybe it was a mistake to mention the biscotti, because Austin was still teasing her about her favorite treats from the bakery when they got to the fire pit and caught everyone listening in. Or maybe they weren't, and it was some other reason that everyone went silent and smirky when she arrived.

Mateo—wearing that particularly tight-across-his-arms purple heather tee she loved—was building one of his famous tent-shaped campfires in the stone pit. Of course it blazed up right away. Sally raised her spiked coffee in a toast to the mighty fire of Mateo, then took Alicia's guitar and began to tune it.

Alicia shook her head at his glinting eyes. She'd run out of ways to bolster all her defenses against the general goodness and goodwill surrounding him. "He builds fires, he fixes fridges. Is there anything that man can't do?"

The tease in her voice made him blush. Or it could be the heat from the flames, but given how he'd ducked his head and regarded her under lowered brows, she suspected a blush.

Sally asked about the fridge, which got Alicia and Abraham telling the story of their near disaster. Most everyone knew about the sale of the building, so they knew how bad it was to be shoveling cash at appliance repairs just then.

"Thing is, we used to be able to have Pat Bowser just come on by for things like that," Mateo said.

Quinn nodded. "I miss that guy."

"We all do," Alicia agreed. "We were lucky that Mateo could help us out, but ever since that big box store pushed Pat out of business, there's no one like that around. Someone we can count on to handle any problem, not just ones like the fridge where we happen to know someone with the right skills."

Mateo mentioned a couple of customers on his delivery run trying to navigate the same situation. Pat had tried to train up a couple of his sister's kids, but one of them ended up in the East Bay doing tech work, and the other one had never come back from her junior year abroad in Spain.

"She came back for a hot minute," Austin said.

Noah laughed. "You would know."

Austin knocked his knee into him. "Shut your mouth."

"So, you weren't enough to keep her around town, I guess. It's no wonder you don't want to go bragging about your exploits," Noah said.

Austin pointedly ignored him.

Mateo filled the conversational gap with the news that Saturn Sandwich Shop's owner had confessed he was being wooed by fast food chain that wanted to buy him out.

"Oh, hell no." Sally stopped strumming. "We can't let that happen."

"Sure, but what are we going to do about it?" Noah flopped back against the blanket, nearly knocking her coffee out of her hand. It would serve him right if she gave him a bit of a scalding on his arrogant face. Damn cousin determined to knock down all their community dreams.

Mateo was squinting. Not against the smoke this time, since it was headed straight off the sea and up towards the street.

"What are you thinking?"

He caught her watching him and shrugged. "Not much, really."

"Lies." She grinned a challenge at him.

He tilted his head. "Just remembering something my dad said about when he was refinancing the bakery, after my grandparents retired."

"Yeah, and what was that to do with?"

"I don't know. You probably don't want to hear this."

Austin sat straight. "Don't want to hear what?"

"It was about the banker we worked with. He accessed a community development fund designed to support locally owned businesses. Back then, Surfside was going through a lot of the same as now. You know, coming out of recession, trying to keep the corporate interests at bay. Obviously that's not still an ongoing thing, or maybe you'd have been able to tap into it for buying your building."

She shook her head. "No, there's nothing like that now, not that I was able to find out."

"We used to do a whole thing with introducing new students to the town during orientation week. It was like a small business fair, from what I remember. Seems like I heard it started up for the same kind of local support reasons." Sally had attended the university before getting herself hired as one of the librarians. "I don't remember them doing anything like that for a while. But I don't know why it stopped."

Mateo was up and alert now. "Okay, so maybe we need to make that happen again. Who can we talk to about it?"

Noah was already shaking his head. "No good, man. I can't even get the council to call me back about Surf Fest, and that's been happening every year for two decades."

She looked from her cousin to Mateo, who slumped back on his elbows in a way that seemed to smash apart the enthusiasm he'd been developing.

She called utter bullshit on that. This inkling of a plan was the first time she'd located a new potential lifeline she could use to turn their luck around. "Maybe you couldn't get the council to deal with you, Noah. But I bet Mateo could."

Her cousin shouldered her lightly enough that her coffee wouldn't have spilled on him if she hadn't made a point of it. She wasn't a jerk—it wasn't still hot enough to scald. But it did stain what she knew was of was one of his favorite white concert tees.

"Hey!"

"Hey yourself." She rested her laser eyes on him.

"Fine." He patted uselessly at the coffee stain. "I'm useless, and Mateo is not. So what's your plan?"

The way she was looking at him. All shiny like he had some superpower he'd never even heard of. Like he could give her the one gift she'd never thought to ask for. His heart pounded loud when she licked her lips and furrowed her brow to begin speaking.

"It's not a plan. Not exactly. Nothing so clear. More like two bits of an idea and a sketch of another. I'm just thinking about the fair. Noah mentioned Surf Fest, and you know those towns that are, like, 'Keep Austin Weird' or 'Keep Portland Cool?' And that's part of the whole appeal of Surfside, right?"

She was looking at Sally, but Mateo spoke up with a memory. "The emails I got from campus back when I enrolled mentioned all that. Unique charm of the town and so on."

"Right," Alicia said. "So that's got to be a draw, right? For campus and for tourism both. People want a Panera, they've got that at San Jose State. But when they want Saturn's Sandwich Shop, and Noah's Surf Gear, and James Family Bakers—"

Mateo interrupted. "And Pier Three Coffee instead of Starbucks."

"Right." She was up on her knees now, shining at him. Every angle of her face was a brighter spark than the fire he'd built between them.

"Okay. So, what? I try to turn this into some sort of movement?" He hoped his voice was steadier than the pounding urge to help her led him to expect.

"I don't know. It's just—there's got to be some way to capitalize on all that."

"Capitalism is always the problem," Noah offered.

"Yes, yes, we know that." Alicia patted his shoulder. "But capitalism being the problem isn't gonna stop Mrs. Vallejo selling to some random property developers."

He didn't like how she sank back into the shadows as her voice trailed off.

"Well, it's maybe not going to stop any number of local businesses getting vultured by larger commercial firms. But ..." He caught himself kneading the hem of his shorts between his fingers, and scrubbed his hands through his hair to shake out his racing nerves.

Sally piped up. "But if it was part of an ongoing effort?"

"Right, that. Make it a rising tide effect." He shot a glance probably too full of apology at Alicia. "I don't know what it looks like, though."

"Maybe—I mean, I might have something." Then she left her own blanket and helped herself to a section of his.

Be still his fucking heart.

"Okay, so maybe we need to brainstorm this." She handed over her cup for him to hold while she settled all her heat and softness and beauty beside him.

Just a brush of her knee against the meat of his calf, and he was head to toe tingles. Ridiculous, when they'd spent so much time being naked, for it to feel so intimate. Half a dozen people watching them and not so much as a kiss between them, but he felt flayed and exposed. And somehow noble, with the way she flooded him with questions about his customers and other local contacts.

Building castles from the sand beneath them. Each one of his answers fortifying walls of some kind of dream they could share. It was like she'd come up with a quest, looked around their circle of friends, and decided that he was the one who could complete it for her.

"I don't get why you think Mateo can persuade all those people, when I'm the one who's been schmoozing council members for weeks." Noah complained.

He didn't either, but he wasn't going to stop Alicia's momentum with those kinds of doubts. She, Sally, Austin, and Quinn kept piling up ideas, and his only goal was to follow their thinking so he wouldn't let anyone down.

She leaned over to look at her cousin, which pressed her shoulder into his. He debated between shifting to shield the bulge in his shorts, or maintaining stillness to keep their contact. "First of all, everyone likes Mateo."

"Hey."

"And," she continued over Noah's protests, "they know he doesn't prioritize his ego over common sense."

"Hey," Noah repeated, laughing.

"He just gets things done. And since he doesn't get caught up in proving he's right all the time, people are happy to listen to him and work with him towards a goal. They know he focuses on accomplishing things, not puffing himself up along the way."

"You are so damn competitive. I'm sorry you're still upset I won the Clash Of the Cousins Tournament back in middle school, but you don't have to be so set in your ideas of who I am now."

Only because they were still shoulder to shoulder did

Mateo realize how sharp that teasing dart from Noah had been. He let his hand drift on top of hers to capture her attention. "Thanks for your confidence in me. It means a bunch. I do have ideas of who to run some of this past. And maybe ..."

He trailed off. Much as he wanted to be equal to her expectations, he had better figure out what he was getting into before he committed. "Well, I'll be exploring some stuff, if you're up for more brainstorming someday."

Alicia knocked back the rest of her coffee and reached across him to take her guitar from Sally. "Absolutely. This could be something pretty big, you know, for a bunch of us, and for Surfside. Thanks for thinking about taking it on."

He settled himself behind her shoulder to accommodate her playing. If she suspected how much more he would accommodate and take on at her behest, she didn't let on. But he didn't need to profess all that at her. As long as she was willing to share her dreams with him, he would do what he could to make them come true.

Chapter Eight

She took a late break to dash up to her apartment and do some cleaning. Not because she was planning, exactly, to invite Mateo up after their meeting. But he was swinging by at the end of his work day, which was the same as the end of her shift, so they could talk with the brothers about some of their Surfside ideas.

If their brainstorming session happened to end with Mateo free to go upstairs with her, what was the harm in bundling up her laundry to stash in her trunk until she could get to the laundromat? She stepped out on the landing, and nearly bashed into Austin.

"Oh, hey, good. Let me in."

"I've got to get back to the counter. Yuji is waiting on me."

"That's okay, you don't need to be here. I just want to go in."

"Are you planning on fouling up my bathroom? Because I gotta tell you, I just wiped down those counters."

He snorted. "It'd serve you right if I did. No, I'm trying to figure something out. Need a few minutes in here to see if it'll work. I'll lock up after."

She made room for him to pass by and headed back to work, wondering what schemes he was playing at now. Not that she'd object to some successful get-rich-quick plan, given that they needed the money for the building, and every best effort of hers had so far failed. But what were the odds that anything Austin came up with regarding her apartment would help them pull together the money to buy out Mrs. Vallejo?

By the time she'd punched out and settled herself at the back corner table, notes lined up neatly in front of her, she was prepared for battle. As soon as Austin slid across from her, she said, "We're not going to make cash fast enough turning it into an AirBnB."

He scoffed. "Obviously. Half a dozen people bought apartments in Mom and Dad's building just to use as short-term rentals. The market's glutted with people who felt too cramped in the cities the past few years, and bought out here to give themselves some space. And now they're all repurposing the properties to be moneymakers. Never mind the negative impact on affordable housing, especially since the recession. They don't care about that when they can have more income for their own portfolios."

"What are we talking about?" Abraham asked, settling into the seat beside Austin.

"Lisha thinks I want to turn her apartment into a short-term rental."

Abraham nodded his thanks as Yuji set a flat white in front of him. "Bad idea. We won't make fast money that way."

"No, it's a bad idea because residential rentals are not a good financial sector right now. We won't make money fast or slow, either one." Austin rolled his eyes like he just couldn't believe his siblings were so uninformed. The brat.

But—probably—the brat wasn't trying to kick her out of her own home. She wished that didn't leave her still squirming like a bucket of bait worms.

No matter what Alicia said, Austin wouldn't reveal his big plan. When Mateo arrived, she tabled the issue and moved on to showing them all the ideas she'd pulled together for a 'Keep Surfside Swell' campaign. She'd gathered info from other towns with similar pushes to keep local flavor intact. Pulled quotes from travel and tourism sites that emphasized all that made Surfside a unique draw for visitors. Tidied up the info Noah had forwarded about what the town council had done in the way of community building incentives. And added her own notes about the council members she'd researched.

"This is—wow, you've really gone all-in on this material," Austin said, leafing again through his copy of her presentation.

Mateo nodded. "It's good work. It really seems like a campaign like this would benefit the town, and suit our community needs, too."

It wasn't that she was glowing under Mateo's specific praise. She just relished a moment of pleasure that others could trace the complex and interwoven threads of a plan she'd put together. It put a shine to her armor, his understanding the situation and offering assistance to enact all she'd dreamed up.

But then Abraham leaned in and tarnished her mood. "I get where you're coming from. And once you and Mateo and whoever pull all this together, set things in motion, I can see it having a positive effect on our bottom line. But, Lisha, that's months, maybe years down the road from now. Even if Austin's plan, whatever it is, managers to net us some quick cash. We're counting down the days until Mrs. Vallejo needs a commitment from us. And that has to come with actual money, not flyers about some future street fair." His palm swept across her presentation notes like they made no difference to the fate of Pier Three.

"So what are you saying?"

"We need to think about letting go of the idea of buying out the lease. I don't know if that's looking for a new place to rent, or ..." He trailed off, but the look Austin gave her said he knew as well as she did that what Abraham wasn't mentioning was them going out of business.

Her throat was full of too many frogs for her to muster up a glare for her big brother. "That is not an option. Not for me."

Abraham's expression didn't change, though Austin tilted his head like he was solving calculus equations with nothing to write on.

Mateo scooched his chair forward a half-inch, managing to also slide it a good ways closer to her. "Abe, there has to still be a chance for you all to buy this place. Alicia hasn't been to every banker yet, right? And this is the kind of thing," he tapped the packet of papers, "that can change someone's view of what makes financial sense. You just have to give them a chance."

She stopped biting her lip. Raised her brows at him. "So we should do this? Turn 'Keep Surfside Swell' into an official campaign?"

He bumped his knee into hers. "You know I love making things official. So, yeah. I'm going to spearhead this just the way Alicia has lined out, and dollars to doughnuts, like we say in the bakery business, it's going to make the difference. Your loan is practically guaranteed."

His beloved had a mission for him, and Mateo's spine thrilled with the knowledge that he could accept the charge.

Of course, she'd thwack his ear if she knew he was thinking such outdated things, so he kept his chivalrous tendencies under wraps. What mattered was that she was giving him this chance. She wasn't shutting him out, wasn't going on about how she could do it all on her own. Wasn't refusing to look at or touch him.

He jotted down some names of people to talk to and made a note to scrutinize the town council and Chamber of Commerce sites. He was pretty sure the woman who ran the bird sanctuary where he delivered bulk bags of seeds on occasion was involved in city planning somehow.

Stealing a glance at Alicia under his brows, he clocked the soft smile she was aiming at his notepad. Valiantly not letting her see him notice, he nodded to the brothers. "If you come up with anything to add, let me know. I want to make this a success. Feels like it could be big."

Abraham's nod was both stoic and skeptical, and he wished he could shield Alicia from the man's attitude. Austin was fidgeting, but not, to Mateo's mind, like he was eager for all this to get underway.

Alicia firmed up that opinion when she asked her younger brother, "Are you gonna tell me what your bigger idea is?"

He drummed his hands on the table, prompting Abraham to reach out to steady his mug before it spilled.

"Oh, sorry, bro." Austin stilled and flipped his attention to Alicia. "I can't let you be the only one with slideshows. Give me a little time and I'll let you know."

"Time is the last thing we have," Abraham reminded them.

Alicia's voice was far from patient when she said, "Yeah, we know. You don't think I've got calendars and spreadsheets and flow charts about all this?"

Austin laughed. "The last thing anyone would think of you is that you don't have a flow chart about something."

"Alicia's famous color-coded, cross-referenced, collated presentations." Abraham's shift to gentle teasing didn't soothe his sister.

"You two can just fuck off," she said, standing. "And you. Want to come up?"

Mateo's grip on his pen was suddenly tight. He looked up at her, ignoring the brothers' snorts of derision. Damn, but he loved when she opened up her space to him. Since neither of them had to work for the next ten or twelve hours, he was not going to be coy about accepting her offer.

"Absolutely. Let's go."

Chapter Nine

She glanced at her apartment, checking that her brother hadn't left anything askew when he'd visited. As far as she could see, it will still neater than it had been in months. For once, she'd turned all of her nervous energy into something productive, getting the place spiffed up while she bolstered herself for their meeting downstairs. She ought to fall prey to nerves more often.

She tapped her hand against the outer edge of her right thigh. She'd had the tattoo artist place a triceratops there, where she could easily reach down to its purple-green flank anytime she needed a reminder of strength. It wasn't subtle, by any means, but it was always effective.

Triceratops-bolstered, and energized by the potential of their plan, she turned a smile full of want on Mateo. The unsteady feeling of not having him as her fuck buddy would soon be nothing but a memory, if she had her guess. She resisted all her urges to fling out her arms and twirl in celebration of everything working out her way, but was spinning and spinning in her head.

"You rocked that," Mateo said, slipping off his shoes to

tuck under the table by her front door. "We're gonna make this work. Abraham's going to be eating his words."

"Hope so."

"I know so. You killed it." He brandished his copy of the presentation her way. "This is, like, saffron and vanilla and cardamom. All the expensive, delectable stuff."

She grinned as he dropped the paperwork on the little half-bar between her kitchen and living areas. He crossed his arms at her. It probably felt to him like he was just crossing his arms across his chest, an everyday move he performed with no thoughts of how it smashed her concentration on anything but his biceps and triceps and all his other ropy curves of muscle.

"Hey, what do you want to put together for dinner?"

She licked her lips. "Oh, you're staying for a while, are you?"

He smirked. "Was planning on working up an appetite, yeah."

"Well, in that case ..." Alicia reached to unclip her hair from the complex system she used to keep it out of her way for working and for facing the beach winds. Once she was freed, Mateo drew her down onto her loveseat and got to kissing. He spread his legs wide to make a cradle for her. She scraped her fingers along his scalp and down the planes and ridges of his shoulders. It was a good few minutes before either of them came up for air.

She rested her head on his chest, and felt perched in a safe place. "I thought you were going to do something about my hunger?"

He laughed. "Just trying to sate a little bit of mine first. It seems only fair if I'm going to cook for you."

She kissed the smile off his silly face. After a bit more groping and fondling and general ratcheting of her nerves to interesting places, he eased her back. "Okay, let me get the soup on for real now. You want to choose a movie?"

"Wow, dinner and a movie. What a generous invitation I extended to you without being aware of it."

"Just because you're smart doesn't mean you got to be a smart ass, A."

"Agree to disagree, Mateo."

Damn, but she made him glow from the inside out. And she'd never admit it, but he could draw his own conclusions about the fact that her little kitchen was fully stocked with everything he needed to make the stew she'd rhapsodized over their first weekend together.

And, okay, they hadn't exactly talked about their relationship. But every one of her actions was telling him she remembered where he was coming from, and meeting him there. Including him in her schemes, the invite up to her place ... he was more than happy to bid farewell to the Alicia who kept walls up between him and the non-sex parts of her life.

An hour later, they were cuddled together, holding bowls in their laps while watching one of the Best Foreign Language Film nominees from the previous awards season. The only way it could be more ideal to him was if the movie were in English or Spanish, so he could eschew the subtitles and spend more of his time watching Alicia.

During one of those instrumental-scored cinematic sequences, she glanced his way. "Why are you looking so gloopy at me?"

"Please explain: what is gloopy in this context?"

"It's whatever this thing is you're doing with," she waggled fingers towards his face, "your brows and your half smile and your tilted head."

He laughed because her attitude always cracked him up. And if she really objected, her hand wouldn't be in the process of smoothing up his thigh.

She rested her bowl on the side table, did the same with his, and straddled him. She didn't know Korean any more than he did, but the way she had her mouth buried in his neck didn't indicate a huge concern for how the protagonists were going to get themselves out of their messy situation.

He yanked her hips closer to his. Encouraged her to grind herself deeper against his hardening cock. The best thing about Alicia's tiny apartment was how easy it was to shift them from the sitting area to her bed. A couple of steps with her in his arms, and they were rolling together on her mattress. Clothes loosening, hands grabbing, worries about fictional characters and bank loans and parental health relegated to some other moment.

What mattered was Alicia, and the way she moved above him, and the way she whispered his name, like it was a dozen syllables instead of three, when he drew her nipple into his mouth.

What mattered was them.

Legs sprawled across the bed, Mateo collapsed against her headboard to gather his breath and gaze at her body. He traced her curves and valleys, rough fingers scraping against the satin of her skin.

"Why are you chilling out right now?"

He bumped up his hips. "The way my cock is throbbing at you seems chill?"

Her hands. She always knew how hard to grab him, how fast to pump. He leaned in for another, more exploratory kiss.

"You are so trying to slow us down," she accused. And because she was right, he didn't bother with denials. He also didn't try to explain. Being welcome in her bed, being cozy in her home—if he articulated how much it meant to him, she'd rush him through sex and show him the door. Never mind accusations of gloopiness; she would see straight through to his longing and his love. And Alicia had yet to signal that she was ready to welcome, much less accept, everything that meant.

Instead of baring his soul, he slowed their lovemaking to an intense and intent rate. Took all the time he—and his balls —could stand, to stroke her from shoulders to shins. To delve his fingers and his tongue into the hollow at her neck. Her navel. Her pussy. To kiss her thighs and her hips and her breasts.

"Mateo," she moaned again, so he drew her up to her knees for better access to her clit. She braced herself on her headboard. He wrapped an arm around her ass and got methodical about licking and sucking her, thrusting his tongue into her slick entrance, thumbing the swollen and tender bundle of nerves at almost the right speed, almost the right pressure. She gripped his hair and he puffed a laughing breath along her folds. She dug her toes into the tops of his thighs, shoving herself faster at his tongue and his thumb.

Finally she grabbed a condom from the table beside her, smacked it against his chest, and demanded, "Stop being a goddamn tease before I fucking murder you, Mateo."

And because satisfying her demands filled his heart, he held her closer and his lips got firmer and his tongue got faster and he worked her diligently until she came all over his face.

She collapsed back to her knees and he prowled over her, nudging her to her back and shoving her boneless legs further apart. His erection really was throbbing, which would make her giggle if she had the energy to do anything but drool at it.

He ripped open the condom packet and she found the motivation to prop herself on her elbows. "Stop."

And he did, because for some good and noble reason she didn't try to understand, Mateo listened to her.

"I want—I need to taste you."

For all the wicked reasons. Because he was so hot and she was so sated. Because the head of his cock was already glistening. Because he'd kissed her tattoo, and growled when she cupped his balls, and her skin still fluttered where his fingers had been.

Because she wanted to.

She slid a tad, to line herself up, and Mateo froze above her. "Don't know if I can last."

"Well, try," she said, and stopped using her mouth for anything as unfulfilling as words. He groaned above her, his ass cheeks flexing under her hand as she kissed up his length and licked down it. Swirling her tongue across the head of his cock, she got lost in the musky-spice warmth of him. The smell and taste of Mateo overwhelmed her, and she only stopped because he finally wrenched himself away to put on the condom.

A desperate second or two later, she'd flipped to her stomach and raised her hips, and thank god that seemed to be enticement enough for him to slide his full length into her aching core. She fisted the covers and arched her back, giving him all the encouragement as he pulled back slowly and surged forward fast.

No idea what she was saying. Too many ideas about what she was feeling. Alicia squeezed around Mateo, and he added cursing to his praise. And reached beneath her to pinch her clit between two fingers, which flooded her nerves so sharply and beautifully that her knees gave out and she flattened to the mattress. Nothing stopped him, though, His cock sliding sure and slick into her, the tap of his fingers at her nub. It was all happening, and happening, and happening so fast, so deep, so so fucking tender and filthy at the same time.

Her body kept gripping him, and Alicia writhed and screamed as everything just came together so sweet and so sexy and so strong. Mateo's thrusts got shorter and sharper and less rhythmic and wilder and she was tipped into another orgasm that peaked as he grabbed her ass and pounded his own release into her.

Chapter Ten

Flushed, and flush against each other. Radiating warmth and soul-strengthening contentment that would look like sunrises and leaping dolphins and rainbows in gif form.

Tucking his pillow under his head, he snuggled her back to his front, and another prism of frolicking puppies exploded in his mind's eye.

His ultimate best life happy place dream.

"My boss grabbed me at Zenon."

All the puppies exploded. His muscles tensed and he forced them to relax because he and Alicia were still so intertwined. So connected. And it seemed like his turning to stone in her bed wouldn't encourage her to keep talking.

"Hmm?"

"I don't talk about it."

"Right. Okay." Was it okay? It wasn't, according to the rampaging wolf in his chest, but of course it was, if that was her choice. He kept up his relaxed and snuggling act.

"That's all. It was just a regular day. No one had been drinking, nothing led up to it. We hadn't even been to lunch yet."

Her body shrank closer to his, and he dared to stroke the part of her forearm his hand rested on.

"I found out afterwards there was a whisper network." Nothing about her voice wavered, nothing suggested she was anything but composed. "Problem was, my boss was new to my department. Zenon moved him to us in the first place because of what people in the other department knew."

"A. Fuck."

"Yeah." She fell silent then.

Mateo's inner wolf was still growling, and he flexed then relaxed his calves and his jaw, to force away a bit of tension. She didn't need to comfort him while sharing her painful truth. "Do you want to tell me more?"

Alicia snorted. "Didn't want to tell you this much. Don't know why I did."

He wasn't going to let the wolf-heart howl in triumph that she'd lowered her barriers and was inviting him in. He was going to lay perfectly still and hold her and plant the gentlest of kisses to the back of her shoulder. "Okay."

"He got fired, anyway. I'm not supposed to talk about it, but, at least in the hospitality business, at least for as long as I was around to overhear things, his reputation was in the dumpster and no one knows it was me. Thing is ..." At that, her voice did jump up with indignation, and she rotated to lay on her back.

Mateo drew the sheet over both of them. "Yeah?"

"They knew. Zenon. They denied it, officially, but that's why he moved departments to start with, because of complaints and rumors. And instead of getting to the bottom of it then, instead of being like, 'yep he's a predator, let's fire his ass,' they just shuffled the problem to us. Gave him a stern warning and some self-study on sexual harassment."

"Jesus."

She turned once more, this time into him. He tugged her

pillow over the top of his, since she liked two pillows and he liked one, so she could rest her head up close to his shoulder. "Anyway. Don't know why I told you."

He hummed an indistinct reply, tucking the blanket behind her, and stroked her spine until long after she'd fallen asleep.

The alarm was not going off, and no one was texting her to complain that she needed to bomb downstairs and open the cafe ASAP. So it took Alicia a moment to grok why she'd woken before dawn smashed its hazy orange all over her ocean view. But then Mateo shifted, presumably not for the first time, and she felt the mattress roll beneath her.

She grunted. "Hey."

He chuckled. "Morning, sunshine."

"If I were sunshine, I wouldn't be up yet," she mumbled, tossing an explanatory hand at the dark windows.

"Yeah, well, I didn't really mean to wake you. Just kinda spent too long laying here looking at you when I should have pulled myself up for work."

"So it's what, four?"

"Quarter till. I'm supposed to pick up some medicine for Marina on my way in."

"Is she okay?" A niggling worry about his sister began to worm into her and wake her fully.

"Yeah, just the usual, nothing scary this time. Means I don't really have time for morning nookie, though."

She pulled the pillow over her head. "Nookie? Are you seventy-four years old?"

His palm on her belly just about burned through the thin cotton separating them. "I beg your pardon. I meant to say, I don't have time to make sensual overtures to my lady fair."

She gripped his wrist to hold it back from further explorations. "Okay, now you're four hundred and seventy-four. That's not better."

"No?" His fingers went just a nice amount of tense and teasing. Enough pressure that she felt them as individual digits, each with its own impish agenda.

"Hmmm. You gonna go down on me before you leave, or are you heading out right away?" She shoved his hand lower.

And like the expert in her anatomy he'd become, he slid straight to her service.

Gorgeous moments later, she sank back against the pillows, replete. "That was nice."

"You're telling me," he said, licking his lips.

She almost didn't even mind his smug tone. "Don't be full of yourself."

"No problem. I'd rather you were full of me."

"Funny."

"One of the many reasons you adore me."

He smoothed her shirt back down to her waist as he scooted up for a kiss. And it was only as he pulled away and got up that she noticed how he'd tugged up her blankets. Was he seriously tucking her in like some tender parcel he needed to care for?

Jerk.

To compound things, his fingers began to straighten the tangle of her hair.

"Thanks for inviting me up yesterday," he murmured. "And letting me stay over. It was a really sweet way to start my day."

She grunted at him, because what else was she supposed to do with that information, or with his gloopy as fuck smile, or the fact that he was goddamn *humming* on his way out the door? The man had gone full lovestruck on her, and she needed to put a stop to it before he started inundating her with flowers and chocolate.

At the thought, she ground her teeth. Two days earlier, he'd shown up with a rainbow-iced devil's food cupcake, just for her. Flour and chocolate. Like she didn't spend all day with access to whichever of his pastries she'd ordered for Pier Three. Like she hadn't spent six years at universities figuring out how to translate her own dreams and desires into a crowd-pleasing business.

Not to mention those years with Zenon, which: she could do without those memories ruining her morning. She'd already dealt with them plenty the night before, and look how that had turned Mateo into Mr. Strong and Sweet.

Drifting back to sleep with the specter of her former workplace glaring at her? Not going to happen. She curled into a ball, willing the past away. The thoughts battered to invade her brain, and burying herself in her tidy blankets did nothing to stop the spiraling.

Damn shame Mateo was halfway to work already; she could use a sex friend to distract her from everything her mind was conjuring up. Then again, if she contacted him, he would go back to being all lovey and protective about her pain. Like she was asking him to fix things, or solve her trauma somehow.

Alicia solved her own goddamn trauma, thank you very much. She solved it by removing herself from the evil, and building her own corner of the world into a place that was not going to actively harm.

Because she was the boss.

She made the rules.

And fuck Mateo if he couldn't work with her on that.

Chapter Eleven

Austin called a meeting, which was strange enough to prompt Abraham to text her directly, instead of their usual method of keeping a three-way chat going no matter who needed to respond or who was being teased.

ABE: Hey you know what this is about?

ALICIA: I'm clueless

ALICIA: Or wait. One clue

ABE: Feel free to elaborate

ALICIA: Might be whatever he wanted to scope out in my apartment for that's not putting it up for rent

ABE: I ran more numbers on that. It's not going to do nearly what we need for covering the payments, even if we could get a loan

ALICIA: Can you remind me where I heard that before? Oh, yeah, when Austin said exactly the same thing before assuring me that he's not trying to kick me out of my place in hopes of a quick payout

ABE: Yeah, yeah. But if he's not trying to rent out your bed, what's he after here?

ALICIA: See previous statement about my not knowing

He sent back an emoji of a seedling, which didn't clear up a damn thing, but at least he seemed to accept that she didn't have any inside information.

When she walked into Pier Three, bypassing a customer in a SuperBean Stance, Cleo offered to make her the latte special. "Yes—or, no, just my dirty chai, thanks." She scanned the cafe. The bright sky, for whatever reason, hadn't beckoned too many customers outside, so she gestured that she would be at one of the empty picnic tables on the patio.

Austin saw her headed that way and followed, stopping to chat with one of their regulars who'd just flopped into the hammock. After he settled opposite her with his neat folders, Abraham slid in beside her, handing over her drink. He launched in, not even clearing his throat first. "It's time to throw in the towel."

She coughed around a swallow of chai that had turned nearly as explosive as her brother's words.

"The hell?" asked Austin. "That is not what we're talking about today."

"We've been running numbers every way I can think of. We can't do it without a loan. And we can't seem to get a loan before Mrs. Vallejo puts it on the market. We give up now."

She made herself sound like she believed in their venture. "We might luck out with a new landlord here. Someone who won't be buying just to knock it down."

"Yeah, we might, but even if they let us keep our lease, they're not gonna turn around and sell to us in three years."

She was glaring at her brother, and he didn't even bother to play like he was sorry for reiterating the depressing points they'd been trading back and forth since they first found out about the sale. She glanced at Austin, who had gone cold in his silence.

Abraham was always calm and implacable, no matter the mood. Nothing ruffled him. But Austin, when he got really mad? It was a few minutes of frozen ire, followed by fireworks.

She kicked Abraham's ankle in warning. He tapped right back at her, like she was the one to worry about.

Another group of customers wandered out and sat nearby.

"Okay, that's it. Let's go." She shoved none too gently at Abraham as she stood up. "If we're having this out, we're not doing here."

She grabbed Austin's papers, because the last thing she needed was him flinging them to the ground while everyone watched. At least they had chains on the picnic table so her brother couldn't flip them. She scooped up Abraham's water bottle and her tea while she was at it, and stormed around the building to her stairway.

In her apartment, she slammed everything down on her coffee table and laser-eyed her brothers. "I don't know why we didn't meet up here to start with."

"Because Abraham's always weird about entering your space."

"Well, it's a nice change from how you barge in any damn time you feel like it, but that doesn't mean it's not asinine."

"Excuse me for respecting your personal space," Abe said, which Alicia could tell wasn't doing a thing to rewarm Austin's cold iron heart. Her brothers shared an apartment, which was a congenial enough arrangement eighty percent of the time, but tore at every one of their differences in personality when they had any serious conflicts.

"Don't start," she told her older brother, taking it upon herself to push them back to work matters. She opened Austin's binder and distributed his printouts between the three of them. "What are we looking at?"

And then her eyes caught up to her hands, and she read

the heading on Austin's proposal: Pier Three Workspace and Production Studios. She flipped the page over and studied Austin's sketches. She looked at her dressing and bed area, which in Austin's rendition, had become two enclosed and soundproofed studios. The eclectic and comfy area where she and her brothers were sitting was replaced by a six-person table, complete with tech ports and a media screen mounted to the wall in place of the painting her college roommate Callie had done for her. Her adorable blue two-person dining table was jettisoned in favor of a printer and some other unidentifiable electronics. The whole thing was sleek black and chrome instead of any of the bright colors or soft textures that she'd spent so long curating into her home above the waves.

Abraham's head was still ducked, so she looked at Austin. "Never mind what I said about barging in. I think I appreciate Abraham's restraint now."

Abe snorted, which was quite emotive of him.

"Okay. So, you're not going to give me a chance to lead in this at all." Austin was folding his body into himself, and any other time, Alicia would give him credit for reining in his temper instead of going off on them.

He took back his binder and handed them each another page she hadn't noticed in her initial rush. "Here's some comps and projections. At the moment there's nothing else like this in Surfside. I know a bunch of guys who are trying to book time with the production facilities up on campus, but their program's going into high gear. They're a lot stingier with renting out the space now that they have so many in-person student users. Plus, there's another whole segment that's ripe for us. You've probably seen how many people try to set up video conferences downstairs, claiming a corner of the space? Hell, a bunch of them are just launching into their Zooms without caring who's sitting right next to them. We can offer them this space for their calls. At the conference table, or in the studios if they aren't booked by podcasters or whoever."

"I thought everybody having their own podcast was a temporary situation and now we're back in," Abraham waved his hand, "normal times, it's all petering off."

Austin shook his head. "No, that's pretty much here to stay, from what I can tell. Plus, with so many companies now embracing telework ... well, I mean, you've seen how many people plant themselves here with their laptops all day long. They're not going into the office, but not working from their homes, either. Even if it's about co-working quietly with their friends, a lot of people are ending up at Pier Three instead of their homes or offices. But the ambience of the cafe can get distracting, so they'll hop up here for a confidential meeting or to take calls. I've come up with pricing structures for private or semi-private access. Scheduled booking or spontaneous booking, discounts based on drink purchases."

Abe pulled out his phone to look something up, which was a sure sign he was intrigued. "What about the cost to convert this place?"

Austin leaned in, flipping the page. "That's all on there. I can do the build out myself, no problem. So it's just the materials."

She snatched the page out from between her brothers' noses. "Excuse me."

They blinked like she was shade who'd appeared in front of them with no warning.

"This is my house. How are you going to convert my bed into a recording studio when that's where I have to actually sleep at night?"

Austin handed another copy of the projection sheet to Abraham, who sat back to study it more closely. "I know, Lisha, but we all want to buy the building from Mrs. Vallejo.

Explain to me how we would be able to do that if we can't get a loan based on our current income."

Abraham got calm and quiet when he was angry. Austin turned cold and exploded. But Alicia—and damn her for falling prey to gendered conditioning—she curled up and battled serious tears.

"Hey, come on, Lisha, come on. Look, it's just, I know you like it up here, and I don't blame you, but we need this. We have to do something, and there's no better use for the space downstairs than what we're doing. We've got to maximize the profit we can get from the building. And my plan is going to earn us more than the rent you pay. Plus, once we get it set up, there's very little ongoing cost associated with it. People are paying us for internet, quiet walls, the chance to do their recordings while they sit in a comfortable chair with mixing equipment instead of scrunched up on the floors of their closets. I already know half a dozen people who are interested, just from running the idea pass them. My friend, Ty, he does audio engineering? He's offered to consult on the setup for us, no charge."

She tucked one of her throw pillows between her torso and her legs, hugging herself into a soft ball. "None of that makes a difference. I mean, not saying you didn't put together good info here, Austin, but no matter what its potential is, you're still kicking me out of my home."

He winced, nodding like he had to deliver bad news. "I haven't run it past Abe, but I was thinking he and I could double up at the apartment, and you could take my room."

Abraham lowered the paper and leveled a look at Austin.

"I know, I know," he said. "I'd have to clean up my act, but I'm asking Alicia to sacrifice this place. So how can I carry on without making some changes of my own?"

If she weren't so busy fighting down tears, she might offer her little brother kudos for not being entirely self-absorbed.

But the tears were a distinct threat, and she couldn't even redirect her attention to her brightly comfortable sitting area or the ever-changing view of the Pacific Ocean outside without feeling like every one of the comforts she'd built so meticulously for herself was being smothered under thick layers of foam insulation tiles.

Chapter Twelve

She swallowed. "I never told you why I left Zenon."

Abraham lowered the paperwork. "Because we had the inheritance after Grandmama died and decided to open a business that would engage us and also help redistribute and build wealth in our community."

She hugged the pillow tighter. "Yes. But, that wasn't everything. I'm not saying I didn't really want to do this." She nodded her chin towards the door like they'd get she was talking about the cafe they'd spent so many years establishing and keeping alive. And really, she was sure they did. Whatever else was stressing their relationship, she knew her brothers, and knew they were in many ways a solid team.

"Something happened," Abraham said.

Alicia didn't need that split-second glance at his face to know he was laying in stores of fury on her behalf. She wished she could reassure him that he didn't need to worry. That his anger was unwarranted. When she didn't, Austin pushed himself to standing and backed up to the wall.

She offered her brothers a halfhearted smile. "I don't feel

bad about talking you into opening Pier Three, for the record."

"Of course not." Austin's eyes narrowed and Abraham's arm crossed his chest in an echo of the way she hugged her knees.

"What happened at Zenon?" he asked. Anyone who didn't know him would think he was barely interested in her answer.

"I signed an NDA," she started. "That's why I never said anything at first. But, it also wasn't ... anything I wanted to talk about. Still don't."

"Lisha. You know you can tell us anything, right?" Austin's damn gentle tone pushed her angry-cry buttons even harder.

"The only thing you two really need to know is how it made me more determined to be my own boss. To not keep ending up vulnerable—I despise that word, but I don't have a better one, so: vulnerable, to whatever power plays and ..." She ducked her head to the pillow so it could absorb the tears she wasn't doing a great job of suppressing. "And harassment that can come with working for someone else."

"You were harassed." Abraham said. It wasn't a question.

She shrugged. Not because she was downplaying it. Because there wasn't so much that she wanted to say about it.

Austin was pacing so stridently he could probably be heard in the coffee shop below. "Somebody—an NDA, so some boss. What? Verbally abused you? Put his hands on you?" He stared. She didn't answer. He spun for more stomping in her space. "Treated you with that kind of disrespect? And you didn't tell us? What the fuck, Alicia."

She watched him storm and bluster while demanding answers to questions that he had no goddamn right to ask. Understanding how he reacted was one thing; putting up with it was another entirely.

Finally, Abraham kicked out a leg to halt him in his tracks. "It was none of our business."

Austin rounded on him. "None of our business? She's our sister, goddamnit. If it's not our business, whose is it?"

She was too curled up to care about answering him just then. But at least Abraham wasn't acting full of male-patterned nonsense. "It's her business. And she didn't want to tell us. That's her business too."

Austin threw up his hands. "So what did you do about it? Did someone lose their fucking job, I hope? Did you get a settlement? Is some asshole out there, acting like he can pressure any young woman he comes across into putting up with his creepiness?"

He was fucking ridiculous. And insulting. Abraham moved to answer, but Alicia didn't need anyone else fighting her goddamn battles. She'd worked too long and too hard to put herself in charge of her own wars. "Like I said, I signed an NDA. Plus, no, it's none of your business. So, I really don't need whatever kind of attitude you're having about it."

Austin paced, unabated. She curled tighter into herself so she wouldn't have to watch his irritation take up space in her living room.

"Why are you telling us now, then? You're not giving us any way we can do something about it. You haven't mentioned this for years, and all of a sudden you need to unburden yourself?"

Now Austin was casting blame at her for a bullshit situation she'd done her goddamn best to survive and put behind her? Disrespecting all she'd done so she could thrive like the badass she was? He was too busy ranting to fall victim to her eye lasers or to notice that his words were target-bombing all her tenderest vulnerabilities.

But Abraham sat forward and planted his hand on the

coffee table. "I don't need you to elaborate. If you need something from us, though, just ask. You know we'll do anything."

Austin frowned. "Of course she knows we'll do anything. That's why she never told us what was happening. She didn't want to give us a chance to act."

"What kind of acting are you thinking of, little brother? You look like you want to solve things with violence, which, newsflash, is exactly the kind of bullshit attitude common to the kind of men who cor—who did that to me."

Then Abraham stood, putting his body between her and Austin. "Did what to you?" he asked. Because, apparently, saying he understood it was her business and acting on that truth were two different things. One hint of something specific, and so much for his mature, considered response.

Thing was, even the thought of 'specific' meant sweat behind her knees and a rumbling shallowness to her breath. So, no. She wasn't falling for his big brother demands.

"Did the thing that I signed a nondisclosure about," she said, her enunciation tight and clipped. "All I'm trying to do is explain to you guys how much it matters to me that I don't have a boss anymore. I know we've all sacrificed other career paths, and put ourselves through seventeen kinds of hell to keep Pier Three going after the past couple of years. And I know I couldn't have done it without you two. Austin, you're amazing at employee relations, and the fact that we've kept our staff for so long is a credit to your management and how you laid the groundwork for collaborative communication. Abraham, your big picture vision is so deep and keen. Without that, we'd probably have folded a year ago, but you've never met an obstacle you couldn't surmount or pivot around."

She gave a small nod at Austin's snort of disagreement. "Or, yeah. It used to be that way. I thought if I could tell you a little about Zenon, maybe you'd get my need to hang on to Pier Three. I'm not gonna stop trying for a loan. I think this community building effort for local Surfside shop owners could work out to something. But you don't think anything we do will be viable. So, I guess, thanks for doing all you two did since we thought up Pier Three. If this is the end ..."

Abe swung away, nudging past Austin. Their younger brother knelt and pointedly gathered all of the papers into tidy piles on the coffee table. Alicia's memory flashed on a photo from when they were all young enough that their age differences were clearly reflected in their heights. Austin, leaning his toddler frame up against her, while Abraham hovered at her other shoulder. Their stair-step of neatly brushed dark hair was a whole world of togetherness away from where they were now.

Austin slumped against her sofa. He tugged away the pillow she was hugging and tucked it behind his head.

She sighed and leaned back, watching Abraham stare out her windows. "I'm not trying to say that it ruins my life if we can't buy the building. I'm really not about emotional blackmail here. Just. I hate the uncertainty. I hate not knowing if our new landlord is going to extend our lease or bulldoze us or raise our rents sky high. I know our strategic vision for Pier Three includes buying this building, and if it weren't for Mrs. Vallejo needing to fund her relocation to be by her kids, maybe we could have done it without any kind of change to the plan."

Abraham moved to lean against her desk. He tilted his chin at Austin's paperwork. "It's not that something like that couldn't work out in the long run."

She bopped her knee into Austin's shoulder. "As long as no one minds kicking me out of my home."

"Sure." He braced his arms on his knees and dropped his head. "Innovative thinking loses again. Never mind. I'm sure you'll come up with some other schemes soon enough."

Abraham wrapped his hand over his opposite shoulder.

"That's the problem. It's coming too late. We don't have time to build up a new revenue stream, or for a community spirit effort to get underway. I talked to Ernesto who I roomed with in college. He's in commercial real estate down by Monterrey, and he says there's enough developers out there right now that if the building goes on the market she'll get competitive bids, fast. Full price or more. It's not gonna drag out and give us time to do all of this petitioning city council and buying noise cancelling paneling stuff. She only gave us this long to come up with our own offer because she knows it'll get snapped up as soon as she signs with a broker."

Alicia nodded. "I'm not trying to keep the woman from her grandchildren. I know Ellen needs her there to help when she goes back to the office full time. I just didn't imagine us flaming out this way."

She caught a flash of wounded pride on Abraham's face and sighed. "It's fine. We'll find out what happens next, and rework our business plan from there. Who knows, we might get lucky and she'll sell to somebody who likes the idea of collecting rent from an independent coffee shop, and nothing much about our daily lives will change."

"And I won't kick you out of your apartment," Austin said.

"Silver linings, great," she agreed.

"Even if the new landlord knocks this place down, it doesn't have to be over," Abraham said. "We can relocate. We don't even have to stay in Surfside."

It was Alicia's turn to snort. "Sure, Mom and Dad would love that."

"I'm not talking Santa Barbara. I was just thinking ..." He waved her hand northward. "Up the coast or something."

"Okay," she said. "Make that your next task. Scour all the towns between here and San Francisco, looking for one that has at least three piers, so none of the work that we put into building the brand will go to waste. Or we can just open a kiosk at the mall and assume no one will ever ask why we're called Pier Three."

She subsided because it had been a long time now since she'd won the debate with Abraham about naming their business after something as site-specific as the pier where they'd gotten a rental agreement with good terms and first right of refusal. Mr. and Mrs. Vallejo had been big on keeping businesses local, so she'd argued for how much it would work in their favor to be closely identified with a popular local destination.

Not to mention the symbolic nature of the name to her. The three of them together, building something strong, something that could withstand tides and floods. Even while telling herself that she was her own boss and not beholden to any of the corporate evil that tried to drag her under at Zenon, she knew she had stability and reinforcement with her brothers. They were all willing to work hard to build a successful partnership, even if they didn't always appreciate each other's contributions and strengths. So she didn't want to give Abraham a chance to say I told you so about the name of their company.

She bit back that particular rant in favor of looking over Austin's proposal again. "Are these numbers for real?"

He moved like he would snatch the papers back from her and she pulled them closer. "Where'd you get these comps?"

"I may not have an MBA, but I'm not unfamiliar with how these things work. You've drummed it into our heads often enough."

"I don't have an MBA." Austin was always acting like he couldn't remember the difference between her Master's in Hospitality and Abraham's degree in business accounting. He conflated them both like it made a difference to either of them that he was eternally twelve credits shy of his own bachelor's degree.

Austin grunted.

"Anyway." She ruffled his hair, because it irritated him and he deserved it after grinding his footprints into her area rug. "It's a cool idea. Maybe even worth making me move, in other circumstances. Not in with the two of you, because nothing's worth that. But cool regardless."

Chapter Thirteen

He hustled to Pier Three after his shift to update Alicia on the latest contacts he'd made. Also because, frankly, he hoped for another overnight with her.

Inch by inch, she'd been making more room for him since they started the Surfside Swell campaign. Added an over-door hook to her bathroom so he could hang his wet towel. Handed him one of her mismatched cups to leave with his toothbrush by her sink. Scrounged up a spare phone charger to plug in at his side of the bed. Even tucked one of the pillows away in a corner, since he preferred to sleep with just one.

He could fetch his own cup and charger. But he relished the gift of her choosing to do those things without his first asking or presuming.

He parked in the customer lot since he hoped to be there long enough to block any incoming deliveries in the morning, and had his notes spread on the table by the time she got through her line of customers and brought over his mocha.

"Busy day?"

"Not bad. Yuji had to take off early, though, so it's just me this afternoon."

"He doing okay?"

"Yeah, just end of semester stuff. So he'll have flex hours the next couple of weeks to be sure he keeps on top of it."

He nodded. "You want to do this later, then? Wait until you have reinforcements?"

She closed her eyes. Pressed her lips together.

His own lips felt dry all the sudden, so he chanced a sip of the hot mocha.

Alicia sighed and eyed him. "Look, I get that you started all this to help us out. But every day closer to our deadline, I have more doubts that I can take any more pressure. We already gave the baristas as many shifts as they want, to spare time for the three of us to work on presentations and beat the bushes for funding. But Yuri and Baptiste have finals, and Cleo can't take on any more overtime. I don't want to leave you in the lurch, and I'm not saying I don't appreciate all of this."

Her gesture at his spread notes looked more dismissive than appreciative to him.

She rushed on without letting him speak. "Thing is, I'm stressed, Mateo. And right now, I feel like you're coming to me for a lot of validation and a lot of accolades. And I'm just not sure I have it in me to pamper you that way. If you're still committed to Surfside Swell, and there's something specific I can do, I will. No question. I haven't stopped thinking it's important for the town, even if it doesn't end up benefiting Pier Three. But my cup's overflowing, and I just don't know that I can take you pouring more into it."

He felt floaty, like he was viewing himself from a misty distance. But also, he was hyper-focused on her clenched hands and the tendons standing out on her neck.

She turned at the sound of the door opening, and his breath caught. Not a conciliatory word, she just turned and walked away.

And yeah, he got it. He worked in the service industry, too. But that didn't mean he was sanguine about the way she called a halt to their conversation. Leaving him with a mocha and scrambled notes spread across the table. He glanced over them, wondering if she was right about him crying out for accolades. Not like he'd ever shown up and said, "Behold my brilliance and praise me."

Sure, he was invested in the Surfside Swell campaign, but it hadn't been his brainchild. She was the one that named it, for fucksake. If she needed a break, she could just say, 'I need a break.' He'd never complain about that. Their whole relationship had been at her speed, so how was she justifying acting like he was a nuisance? The campaign started because the bonfire gang had been talking about her business problems, and now everything he'd done to bring her some relief from all that pressure of hers was bothering her?

From behind the counter she flashed him a half grimace, half smile, but only stopped chatting with the customers who'd settled in to await their drinks to hop to the pass-through window and remind a surfer to use the grey water tap to spray off his board.

He was knocking back his mocha and debating his next move when his phone trilled with Marina's ring tone. She rarely called him, especially if she was already home from school.

"Riri, what's up?"

"Matty?" Her voice was pitched high, and his pulse jumped to match. He was already scrambling his damn notes into a pile to shove into his pocket while he waited for her to continue, and was halfway to the car by the time his sister took a gasping breath and rushed out, "Papi. He's had an attack, a stroke, I think? I don't know what ..."

"Where are you? Where is he?"

"The shop. The ambulance is here. I—"

"Hang on, hang on, I'm on my way. I'm driving. Is Mom there? Is Sean or somebody who can lock up the place?"

"Okay, good. Yeah, Eleanor's here, I'll ask her. She ... yes, yeah, we're all here."

"Should I meet you at the hospital?" He looked at the console like the bluetooth and GPS could tell him what he needed to know. Bakery in three, four minutes. Hospital would be maybe eighteen. "He's alive, Marina, right?"

"Yes, sorry. He's alive. He is ... he fell in the kitchen, but there's no blood."

"Tell him I'm on my way. Where should I go?" Maybe if he gripped the steering wheel tighter he could pull himself together enough to be there for his sister. "The bakery? Dad's alive, and Mom's there, and the ambulance is there."

"Yeah." One little syllable, but still Marina's voice wobbled.

"And Eleanor is there. So, ask her can she lock up."

"Okay."

"Go on. Do that now, let's get that sorted."

"Right, yes. Okay. The paramedics ..."

"Okay, one thing at a time. We can do this. We got this, Riri. Check with Eleanor." He swerved through an intersection to cut his way back towards the shop. It was closer than the hospital. Mateo needed to wrap his arms around somebody in his family as soon as possible.

Marina came back to him. "She's fine. She said she can do it."

"Okay, good girl. Good, thank you. Look, I'm two minutes away. Less. Okay? I'll get there and then we can head to the hospital. Just hold on for me."

"Okay, but drive safe, Matty."

"I am, I swear. I promise."

Marina sniffled and it nearly cracked him open. It was that floaty feeling from talking to Alicia, but ten times as intense.

In the back of his racing mind, he noticed his foot was hurting, and it took long moments to realize all of the toes on his left foot had curled up on themselves.

He got close enough to see the ambulance, which meant he was close enough to grab a parking space and run for the bakery. Mr. Walters was standing on the sidewalk outside of his firm, looking like he wanted to ask a question.

Mateo shook his head. "It's Dad, I don't know," he blurted and ran past.

The flashing ambulance lights might as well have filled the interior of the bakery as he moved through it. Information came at him in flashes. He took in that they were low on ciabatta rolls but barely registered Eleanor behind the counter. One of the paramedics was wearing a green hat but he couldn't tell anything else about them. Mom was wringing her hands, and that was all he could focus on for the few seconds it took for him to reach his family. Once his arms were around Marina and Mom, everything stilled around him.

He stared the gurney. "Hey, Papi."

His dad encouraged him as he was wheeled past. It was more a lift of the eyelids than a smile. But he knew what it meant.

It meant, "Be calm, Matt."

And, "Don't make a fuss, Matt."

And, "Make sure everything's taken care of, Matt."

Because that was the bargain they'd made. Mateo would never have to fight to be accepted as someone who had broken the James family mold, as long as he was always going to be around to get things done.

He nodded at his dad, squeezing his mom closer so the paramedics could get by. "You want to go with them, or have me drive you?"

Mom rubbed his back. "He'll be okay, mijo."

It wasn't what he'd asked. But he soaked up every scrap of

her comfort, even while he knew it was wrong of him to look to her for reassurance. She was the one whose spouse was on the way to Surfside General.

"You drive us."

He nodded and steered her and Marina out to his car. Mr. Walters was already in the street, waving traffic to a standstill so the ambulance could head off. He kept the cars at bay until Mateo had swung out behind the EMTs. Mom held his hand, and Marina leaned forward, gripping both their shoulders, for the whole of the drive.

Chapter Fourteen

He'd just walked out without saying goodbye.

Her fault, obviously, since he hadn't exactly invited her to dump all of her stress on him. He was just keeping her informed.

Okay, maybe some of what she'd blurted about him always looking for her approval was true. At least he wasn't doing it in that way of some guys she'd dated, where they didn't even notice an empty fridge, but expected her to thank them for helping to put everything away once she made a list and bought the groceries.

Mateo wasn't leaving her to do the mental labor of the campaign and asking for cookies when he did the tasks assigned to him. He was invested, and it was wrong of her to treat him like that aspect of everything was a problem. He also didn't balk at taking direction from her. Didn't treat her like her strong ideas were weak, and her super strong ideas were actually his. The way he praised her straddled the line between acceptable and embarrassing.

But nowhere in their dynamic of his craving her approval

would she have figured him for the kind of guy who would just walk away while she was serving customers.

Since she was alone until close, she didn't have a chance to duck out and call him. She texted a couple of times. No response, which was just more fuel to her ire. She was washing out the equipment and debating if she was obliged to seek him out and find out why he'd bailed so hard when she'd only lost her temper a little, when Abraham came in.

"You're still here."

"Obviously."

"Thought you'd have Yuri close up. I was coming by to help him."

"No, he's got finals. Why are you so surprised? I'm on the shift schedule."

"Yeah, but I thought you'd take off with Mateo."

She shut off the water. "What are you talking about?"

"His dad is in the hospital. I figured you'd be with him."

"What happened? Is he okay?" She grabbed her phone and checked her lack of notifications again. "He didn't tell me."

Abraham moved closer. "Sorry, Lisha, I thought you'd know. From what I heard it's his heart."

She was patting down her pocket for her keys and stripping off her apron. "Shit, I gotta get over there."

He hooked her arm when she tried to move past. "Listen, breathe. You're wiped out from the day. You're a mess, and you need to get ahold of yourself before you try to drive anywhere. Go take a shower or something."

"God, nobody cares what I smell like."

"It's not that you are imbued with espresso, though you are. You're in a panic right now, and I don't want you to drive while you're in a panic. Look, I'll make up a couple of thermoses of coffee and some sandwiches for them. You get cleaned up. You can't give comforting hugs if you smell like coffee grounds and flop-sweat."

She let out a little laugh that deflated some of her panic. "Okay. Yeah, thanks." Another deep breath. She gestured at the cafe. "You can finish?"

"Of course."

"Thanks."

He kissed her forehead, which seemed to surprise him as much as it did her. She dashed up the stairs so she could shower and change. At her door, she stopped. There was a James Family Bakers tote bag hanging on the knob, a bouquet of yellow and orange flowers bursting from the top like they'd captured the colors of the sunset beyond her door and concentrated them into their blooms.

Her hand was shaking as she unlocked her door and slipped inside. The bag also held a bottle of wine and a tight roll of Mateo's spare clothes. He must have left it all at her door before he came in for coffee, hoping to spend the night with her again.

She crumpled her hand in her shirt, thinking of the plans he'd laid before she laid into him earlier. And how much everything had changed for him that afternoon.

Abraham was right. She needed a shower. Mostly she needed to let a few tears escape, so she could show up for Mateo and his family. She was determined to be a support to them, not demand they give her comfort. So she had to banish her tears down the drain.

A few minutes later, she'd wrapped her wet hair in a bun and scampered back down the stairs. Her brother had everything packed up for her, cleaning while he waited. "God. Sorry, you hate sweeping."

He shrugged. "It's not gonna kill us for this place to have less than spotless floors for one night. You feeling more in control now?"

She tapped at the triceratops hidden under her leggings. "Yep."

"Okay then. Let me know how he is."

"Thanks for bringing me the news." She nodded a little, fighting for resolve.

"Hey." He pulled her into a hug and tipped his chin towards the door. "You got this, Lisha."

She gave him a wave, and was off.

For hours, they'd been shrinking into a corner of the ICU waiting room. He sat in an unevenly stuffed armchair, his knee almost touching Mom's where she and Marina huddled together in a plastic-looking loveseat.

He wanted to transform into a giant to be reckoned with. A towering presence wreathed in flashing beacons, dragging every cardiologist in the Bay Area to gather round his father and fix whatever was wrong. And once they'd use their magic cardiology powers to fix Papi, his overwhelming force would compel them to add that much more science to their magic. Make it so this was never going to happen again. So that Papi's heart would tick on healthfully forever. Or at least until a reasonable old age, like ninety, or a hundred and ten.

Instead, every minute they were left alone in their corner, with no updates, no gently smiling person in scrubs approaching them to deliver good news, he was sure they were shrinking. All three of them, but mostly him. Along with their mismatched seating and the scratched-up table between them and the carpet the exact shade of his Papi's crusty rye bread.

They had maybe fifty seconds before they shrank into motes too small to see, when noise crashed over him from the far side of the waiting room.

Alicia entered, large and loud. And the last thing he wanted to deal with.

Marina threw herself at Alicia for a hug. It nearly slayed

him. His sister absolutely vibrated with tension and need in Alicia's arms. Frankly, it infuriated him.

If Marina needed a giant comforting hug, what did she think his arms were for? He'd spent more years than he'd ever wanted to baking bread, and it looked like he was going to continue to for the rest of his life. The one thing that was good for was giving him arms that were capable of massive reassuring hugs. Instead, Marina went and threw herself at Alicia, whom he thought she barely knew. And he was left sitting alone in his lumpy armchair, useless. No one asking of him the one thing that he was capable of giving.

The one thing that would stop him from shrinking into invisibility in this goddamn chair.

Could be the whole room was full of people who needed hugs, not just Riri. Mom could need a hug. He could need a hug. But instead of giving him a chance to be a tiny bit useful, his sister went off and burrowed herself into Alicia's arms.

And Alicia held her up, not the least thrown off by the weight of the bags she was carrying or the press of his sister's trembling body. If he hadn't been frozen to the chair, he'd have stormed over to demand the woman let his sister go. Take her hugs someplace they were wanted.

Not here.

Not now.

He was the one that would give out any hugs necessary, because it was the one and only thing he was good for.

Chapter Fifteen

She wrapped her arm around Marina's shoulder and walked her to the corner where her family sat. She bent to kiss Ms. James's cheek and reached her hand out to Mateo. He didn't take it, which left her hiding a wince. It really wasn't the time to discuss anything about their relationship—friendship, whatever it was. "I'm real sorry about Mr. James. Have you had any news?"

"Thank you, dear. No, we're still waiting."

She nodded and turned to the one offering she hoped would be welcome, no matter how Mateo felt about her. "We packed up a couple of sandwiches and smoothies for you, and here's a carafe of Kona blend." She would have put it on the side table between the family, but given Mateo's refusal to budge, she dragged over a coffee table and laid it all out for them.

"Oh thank you, Alicia. You are an angel." Ms. James's sincerity might have warmed her more had Mateo acknowledged her at all. Still not about her, she reminded herself, and gave the woman's hand a squeeze.

"It's the least we could do. I just wanted you all to know

that we're thinking of you. And if there's anything we can do to help ..."

Marina was reading the labels on the smoothies. "If you come again, can you bring me some of that beet juice one?"

"Riri, that's rude."

Far be it from her to contradict the man the one time he spoke to her. But she nodded. "Of course."

Ms. James wasn't paying any attention to the interplay. But Alicia knew how she liked her coffee, so she fixed her a cup and, whether Mateo liked it or not, leaned over to place it on the side table before taking her leave.

Mom shook herself out of her silent stupor as Alicia reached the doorway. "Mateo, walk her out."

He shook his head. But all that got him was one of her silent looks, this one saying, 'That woman brought us sustenance and kind words; you don't turn into a statue while she departs.'

And since it was Mom, and Mateo made a practice of doing what Mom wanted, he followed her. "Thanks for the coffee," he got out as they watched the elevator buttons flicker information at them. "It was nice of you."

She shifted so she was facing his profile. From the side of his eye, he clocked that she was still and placid and devoid of intentions he could decipher. "I know it's not a lot. But we wanted to be sure you know we're thinking of you."

He nodded. That 'we' of hers was doing a lot of work. And he wasn't sure he understood it.

The doors slid open. The elevator car was empty. In a different situation, he would have stepped into it with her. Taken the opportunity to spend a few more moments breathing her same air. Something in her glance suggested she expected that of him. He didn't budge.

By the time he'd lifted a hand in farewell, her expression had cleared to neutral. She licked her lips. "Let me know when you hear something?"

The elevator doors were shut before he nodded his assent.

She knew Mr. James was out of the hospital.

She knew Sean and Eleanor and the other bakery employees had pulled together enough skilled coverage to keep her orders coming in, and their own doors open during normal hours.

She knew Marina was back in school and Mateo was in the kitchen every morning.

She knew, in other words, the same stuff as every other person on Sean's delivery route. And it seemed it was permanently Sean's now. With Mr. James out for a couple months at least, Mateo had stepped into the gap as head baker. She knew that was what Mr. James wanted, and the last thing that Mateo did.

All this knowledge did fuck all to grant her any power to do anything about it. Mateo had texted twice in the past week. Both messages were to the bonfire group chat. Nothing directly for her.

It was some real letter of the law bullshit, keeping her informed without letting her close.

So she did what he clearly wanted, and stayed away. She quashed her urge to show up at his apartment, or to drop by the bakery for lunch, or to call him when she was flopping alone in her bed at quarter to four in the morning, knowing he was out there starting another day with no plans to see her.

So, that was fine. She was managing just fine on her own.

She'd spent too much time recently ripping herself apart to prove to her brothers that was how she liked it. No reason to throw all that work into the ocean now.

They called the staff together to update everyone on the lack of progress she'd made with Surfside Swell, and the bank meetings.

Austin's leg was dribbling impatiently throughout. Abraham took the opposite tack, barely moving from where his leaned against the back wall, hand shoved deep into his pocket. She stood, restless, between them. "So, our deadline is next week, and after that, we'll be up against the market forces. I don't know how that's gonna go, but I'm not thinking it'll be long before Mrs. Vallejo has a contract. After that, it's up to the new landlord, if they're going to break the lease or keep us going. There's not a lot we can do until then, except keep up our work. Abraham's got some feelers out about new locations. But we've got to take into account that means its own set of expenses."

"We're not thinking of leaving Surfside, though?" Ruthie asked.

Alicia shook her head. "I don't think so. It's something we looked into, and we can discuss it, but I think it's better to try to keep our existing customer base. And for all of us to not have to add to our commutes. Well, all of you. I'm in for a rude awakening."

That earned her a ripple of laughter that lightened the mood just a fraction.

Austin furrowed his brow in sad apology her way. Meanwhile, Abraham didn't shift but somehow became even more still.

"If anyone has thoughts or wants more input about a new location, set up a meeting with Abraham. Thanks, everyone. That's all I've got for now."

It wasn't long before she was closing her door behind

herself. Seemed like everything and nothing was happening simultaneously, and Alicia couldn't find balance between the two. She unfurled her yoga mat on the balcony and told herself sternly to relax and let the sunset and the ocean breeze wash over her while she settled into movement.

Twenty minutes later, she'd tricked herself into a clearer head and heart. Not clear enough to know what brilliant move would put the coffee shop out of danger, but her mind was no longer whirling quite as fruitlessly. After showering, she gathered her notes and sent a few more emails. Futzed with a few more lines in her spreadsheets. Researched a few more progressive investment funds.

Checked her text exchange history with Mateo a few more times.

Well, every other path of her life was rife with landmines; why not take steps down the dangerous road of her raw-hearted relationship?

ALICIA: I've been thinking of you and your dad and everyone

ALICIA: Glad he's home now, hope he's feeling more like himself

The silence continued. No read receipts, no little dots of composition.

ALICIA: I can come by sometime if you want

She set the phone at the edge of her desk and waited, clicking uselessly among the too-many tabs she had open. She caught a notification flash in her peripheral vision, but it turned out to be a news alert.

ALICIA: Maybe you don't want to deal with it right now, with me? And I get that

ALICIA: I get that you've got a bunch going on and I'm not a part of it all. Just want you to know I'm thinking of you, and your family, and also I want to talk to you when you are up for that

Her eyes glazed to dullness as she clicked at her browser, engaging with none of the content in front of her. And no matter how long she forced herself to not send any more messages into the void of Mateo's phone, she never heard back from him.

Chapter Sixteen

He showed up at her door half an hour after her shift was over, because, he supposed, that's just who he was. Somebody asks for an appointment to yell at him, and he obliges, no matter how inconvenient it is to his schedule. Or to his heart.

He was the accommodating guy, the guy who didn't hold on to grudges. The guy who noticed what you needed, and helped you get it. So that made him the guy who knocked on her door after she would have had enough time to decompress from her workday and change into clothes that didn't smell like coffee grounds.

She masked her surprise and ushered him in quickly enough. "Oh, you look tired. Sit down. Can I get you something? Beer, wine? Water?"

The optimist that was his mind gave a tug at his heart, suggesting she wasn't just being solicitous. That he was allowed a flash of joy and gratitude to be fussed over like his welfare was important to her.

But then he remembered her text, essentially demanding he drop everything going on with his life in order to hash out their problems. "No, I don't need anything."

"Tell me about your dad. And how are you, and everybody? Are Marina and your mom holding up? Did Marina get the juice I sent over? Sean said he could keep it cool until he got back to the shop."

"She did. And my dad's got a good recovery plan. Everything's under control. We're just busy, Alicia."

She nodded. "I know. I'm so sorry. I know the job is taking up all your time."

He shook his head. "Is what it is."

She finally moved close enough to make him wonder what was really on her mind.

He was probably dehydrated. Her scent flowed over him and soaked into his pores. "We should—"

She cut him off by sitting down, right up against him, and running her palm across his shoulders and neck. He desperately wished the move didn't have the power to make him long for impossibilities. Not now, when it had finally gotten through his skull that Alicia didn't want to give him more than the lines she drew, back when they barely knew each other.

He'd asked every way he knew how: overtly, and through action, and in the silent intimacy of their bodies coming together.

None of it mattered.

She wasn't interested in commitment, and his constant presence was nothing but a burden to her. Look at the way she was working so hard now to present the aspect of loving partner, and how it was so clearly making her uncomfortable.

No matter how it sliced through his heart with a dull bread knife, the right thing for her, was for him to let her go.

He shifted himself to the armchair, so his body wouldn't be the driving force in how they communicated. "I'll get used to the routine of running everything soon enough."

"You shouldn't have to, though."

She was luring him away from the point. He shook his head to redirect himself. "We'll figure it out."

She clasped her hands, trapping them between her knees. "I know you will. Listen, I don't want you to spend any time worrying about the campaign. I've got it under control. Quinn said they'd optimize the website and make it pretty. And Sally has a ton of marketing and promo stuff drafted already for me to look over. I think everything's in hand."

Right. Because the campaign and keeping her cafe were the most important things to her. "I didn't come here to talk about Surfside, Alicia."

She opened her mouth, then pressed her lips together, nodding for him to continue.

"I know you've already put yourself firmly in charge of everything that's important to you. That's just what I'd expect. Even if I do wonder why it is you can partner up with your brothers and get collaborative with Quinn and Sally, but the minute I'm involved, we're in a battle for control that I never asked for. You even want to control how much I give you. If I don't share enough information, you want to know why. And if I hand over a pile of detailed notes, you accuse me of asking for validation."

"I know. I shouldn't have—I'm sorry."

"That's not the point. I can't be working on Surfside Swell right now anyway. So, you get to be as in charge of everything as you want without me getting in the way." He couldn't look at her dark eyes flashing at him. Everything about being in her space hurt, and the worst pain was the visceral feeling of her processing his words.

She wanted to protest, he thought, but was stuck in 'be nice to the man with the sick dad' mode. He wondered if she was beginning to realize how often she took the emotional lead in their relationship. Well, he was there to spare her any more introspection.

"I didn't come over to talk about the campaign, but I'm glad you've got it under control. I'm sure you'll all do great." He swallowed roughly and shifted so he wasn't looking so directly at her, or her bed, either one. Not that that gave him many options, but he had to protect himself somehow. "I'm reevaluating, I guess, what with everything. And I know I've asked before for you to give me more. And you couldn't. That's fine."

He shook his head, because downplaying his own emotions wasn't his preference. "I mean, it's not fine, not for my heart, but it is what it is. You've been honest. I can't expect anything more than honesty. And that's what I'm trying to give you now."

"Mateo—"

"Please let me talk. I'll just—I'm trying to say I'm done asking you for more. I have to do what's right for me now. Even though it's ..." He found himself staring at her again. His eyes were burning. "It's not easy, Alicia. It's not what I thought would ever say, not to you. But the thing is, I can't keep trying to force a way for this not-a-relationship of ours to fit in my life. It's not working, in too many ways. I'm just tilting at windmills, and I can't do that right now. Can't do it maybe ever."

She made some kind of noise, but he couldn't listen to it. Couldn't do anything but stare at his knuckles and get through the rest of what he needed to say.

"I'm going to head out. But I want you to know, I'm always gonna think the world of you, Alicia. I just don't think I can be part of that world right now, except as a friend. There's too many things I have to focus on." He noticed he was clasping his own hands in an echo of her. Classic Mateo: following Alicia's lead again. There he was, sitting there waiting for her to react before he left, when he was the one who'd come over to say his piece.

At her command, yes. But he'd been the one with something to say. And he'd said it. He scrubbed his hands through his hair and stood, which seemed to jolt her out of her own seat.

"Mateo, hang on."

He retreated towards the door, Alicia close behind him.

"I know you get what I'm saying. I need space to deal with everything in my life right now, and that includes you. The way things stand, you're a stressor to me. It doesn't mean I don't value you. I'm always going to value you. But this," he waved to indicate the narrow space between them, "I can't right now. I maybe can't ever."

Chapter Seventeen

Sometimes she stood barefoot at the water's edge, the wind whipping her clothes, nostrils full of the brine on the breeze, tickled by the foam digging out spaces for each of her toes in the wet sand. When she did that, even the sea birds and the calls of other beachgoers faded against the noise of the waves turning and thrashing right in front of her.

Other times, she was curled up in her apartment with a blanket over her ears and the wind was outside blowing out to sea. As close as she still was to the ocean, it became a muffled presence that she had to concentrate her awareness on.

Mateo talking about no longer including her in his life was like one of those muffled days. She understood what he was saying, but normally when she was with him, every sense was engaged. Now she was reduced to just her hearing, and even it didn't feel as reliable and active as normal.

She had the impression she should say something, but her mouth was dry and her eyes were wet. She cleared her throat. "I haven't meant to be a burden on you."

"It's not that."

"No, sorry." Her hand lifted just an inch, but it stopped

him. "I didn't say that so you would have to jump in and reassure me. That's really not ... my roommate Callie said to me once, back in college? I'd just broken up with this guy who lived down the hall. He kept coming by to rehash the relationship and where he went wrong or whatever, and finally she told me that it can't be the job of the one who ends it, to help process the feelings of the dumped person about the break-up. It never can work. I wasn't the right person to help Wallis then. And you're not going to be the right person to teach me how to get over you now."

He started like he was gonna move to her, but ended up backing another step closer to the exit. When he crossed his arms, it was less the usual enticement to her lust, and more like he was giving himself the hug that she was craving.

"What I'm trying to say is, I should have understood that you never put yourself forward to work on the Surfside campaign. I acted like it was a given. That just because you were telling us about the history, because you inspired it and you know a few local business people, you would automatically be involved in the work we're trying to do. I roped you in without asking first. And that wasn't fair of me, even before everything got so complicated for you with your dad's health."

They stood in utter silence for a moment. Then she braved up enough to push on. "So, I hear everything else you're saying, and I'm not going to hold you up any longer. But I wanted to make sure I said that before you go."

"Alicia."

She tried to smile, because what was more normal than people calling her by her full first name? Nothing, that's what. It shouldn't sting that she might never hear him call her 'A' again.

She set aside how both her stomach and her mood had plummeted with each move away from her he made. First from the loveseat to the chair, now from the living area to the hall. Good thing there were solid floors on this converted bait shack she called home, or she would be plunging right through to the coffee shop.

Mateo pulled his arms tighter across his chest, damn him. Damn him for his reasonable feelings, and damn him for just accepting the reality she'd insisted on. Damn him for looking so beautiful and torn up, like if she would just offer him everything he wanted, he might stop flying apart like a tattered kite in the wind.

And all she would have to do, to make that happen—to reel him back to ground and sew up his torn bits—was to give up on herself.

Alicia was so fucking sick of people asking her to give up on herself.

Suddenly, she was awash with a feeling that if he didn't vacate her place, she would stomp so hard that the integrity of the floor joists wouldn't make any difference to how readily she could crash down to the floor below.

"It's fine," she said, not even sure what she was responding to. She made it easier for him to leave her—leave her space— retreating to lean against her kitchen counter.

There was clearly no point in prolonging his visit. He'd said his piece, and she wasn't in the business of dumping her own messy emotions on someone who couldn't do anything about them.

Even if she wanted him to.

She would deal with it herself, just like always. One thing she'd had to learn over and over—so many times that it was almost natural for her now, almost didn't strangle her esophagus and sink fangs all up and down her legs—was doing things on her own.

When a woman had skills like hers, it was a really, really good idea for the men around her to leave her to it.

Mateo did that thing where he gazed at her for far too

long, like he wanted to jump in and solve all of her problems, stated and unstated. The more fool him, since he just finished telling her how he didn't have room in his life for her problems.

She wasn't going to point out the hypocrisy. He could damn well stifle his gallant urges around her. Could go home and wrestle with them in all the time he'd freed up by ending their arrangement. That worked just fine for her.

Or it would. Once he cleared out of her way.

Finally, he stopped eyeing her like he intended to read her mind. "If there's anything the bakery can do for Surfside Swell, you know we will."

It was like he literally could not stop trying to insert himself into her life, even while he was breaking off their intimacy. Yet another instance of him not accepting that while they had a great physical connection, she had never once asked him for anything beyond that.

She'd gone out of her way to remind him that she didn't *want* anything beyond that.

So why was he standing in her hall, acting like he'd ripped up her heart and he was callously refusing to fix it, she couldn't imagine. As for the ridiculous impulse she had to draw him close and fold her arms around him, that was an inconsequential habit she would get over.

Just like she'd gotten over other people, other lovers and other friends. Other disappointments.

"Okay. See you at bonfire, I guess," he said.

She tried to hide the flinch that whipped through her at the idea of lounging around on the beach with him. She didn't correct him. He could go to bonfire all he wanted to. She lived steps from the waves, and could immerse herself in the surf during any of the many other hours when he would not be there.

Chapter Eighteen

She'd been to two more lenders with no success. Or that was the news he'd picked up between Sean's tidbits and once when Noah stopped by and he'd been working the counter.

And, okay, he'd been texting with Abraham about the new appliance repair guy he located, and happened to ask. There wasn't any reason not to ask. After all, they were still friends. He was friends with the whole Wells family, really. And just because every hour of his day demanded his physical presence at the bakery or at his parents' house didn't mean his mind stopped wandering.

So, he knew about the lenders. And he knew about Noah's discovery that one of the city councilors was retiring suddenly. And he knew that Quinn had set up an interest form on the Surfside Swell website and they were all excited and impressed by the number of people who had signed up.

None of that information made much of a difference to his new daily life. He spent all of his time reviewing bulk orders and running payroll and organizing promotions. It didn't leave him latitude to respond dynamically to anything happening in the world outside of James Family Bakers. It certainly didn't leave him time to contemplate all the holes in his gut that couldn't be filled by bread or work or his love for his family.

Friday after school, Marina showed up and untied his apron as she walked past him.

"Hey." He tried to growl but had to laugh instead. Something about his sister always made it impossible to even pretend she was irritating him, no matter how teenage she got. Or maybe her teen-ness made him even less likely to be irritable with her. When he'd moved out after college, she'd been just coming into some kind of recognizable personality. Now they saw each other mostly at the bakery in early morning quietude or day-end fatigue, but each bit of snark she shot his way was like a dusting of warm spice blooming to life in a rising dough.

"You should go take a nap," she said.

"Wow. Harsh."

"It's not an insult. But you've been here all hours and you've got bonfire tonight. I can stick around and close up."

"I don't have time for bonfire."

"You do if you leave now and go take a nap."

"You woke up at the same time I did and you had a big exam today."

Marina smoothed an apron down her front. "Which I rocked. Now go. I don't want to think about school for at least twenty-two hours, so this is just what I need for a mental reset. I can sleep in tomorrow, and you can't. But you can take a nap now and go to bonfire when you wake up."

Damn if the kid didn't think that just cause she'd grown to almost his height over the past year, she could get all bossy pants on him now. It was like she had no respect for the reasons he was filling every one of his hours with the bakery or checking in on their dad.

He balled up his own apron and tossed it in the laundry

bag. The problem with Sean was, his bits of gossip and speculation never stayed between the two of them. Marina probably knew more about his reasons than was any of her business, and was being oppositional his way because she could.

He tugged at a lock of her hair, and then, before she could protest too much, gathered all of it up into a low bun just the way she liked. He could almost hear her rolling her eyes as she muttered her thanks.

He muttered his own right back at her and held her in a hug that warmed him, but still didn't plug those empty gaps of his. "Text me if you need me."

She shoved him towards the back door. "Yeah, yeah. Make the most of it. This is the last time I can work until after finals."

He sat in the parking lot, limbs loose like they had lost their animating strings. Temps had risen in a way that meant that, by sunset, the air would cool but the sand would retain the day's heat.

He craved that residual warmth. And he had told Alicia he would see her at bonfire. Even if she'd never confirmed she would be there, too. So not showing up, especially when Marina had gone out of her way to give him this chance, would paint him as churlish. His mom messaged that she didn't need him to stop by. And, damn, was he fucking tired of filling his brain with bakery-boss info.

He found himself doing exactly as Marina had mandated.

Austin was at the bonfire ring, acting like a squirrel because Leyla had her head thrown back laughing with Sally. Abraham was there in board shorts and a t-shirt and no prosthetic, a sign he was planning to get so loose that he'd end up laying flat out in the sand before the night was over. And probably stumbling to the Pier Three patio and crashing out on the hammock until the sun woke him.

Quinn was the one building the fire. Noah was the one

hauling a cooler of beer. Jaxson posted up with a couple of old towels for everyone to sit on. Everything proceeded like it didn't matter to anyone that Alicia wasn't there.

He started to plant himself next to Jaxson, until he clocked the way he was eyeing Quinn. So he pivoted to land between the Wells brothers. Unfortunately, that left him facing the Pier Three building, and the faint glow of light from Alicia's apartment.

She was there.

He could tell.

She was there, and not planning to join their group on the beach.

He studied Abe's face in the fading daylight, wondering if the shadows below his eyes were echoed—or amplified—in his sister's face.

"Bad day?"

Austin cracked open a beer and slurped off the foam before passing it to Mateo to pass to Abraham, who grunted.

Suited him. He was in a grunting kind of mood his own self.

He was maybe one beer further into the evening than he should be, given that he wanted to swing by his parents' house before heading to the bakery in the morning, when he heard Sally explaining Surfside Swell to Leyla.

"But it all started because they're trying to buy the Pier Three building, right?"

Beside him, Austin went still in his coiled-spring way. "You know about that?"

The look she gave him wasn't quite pure pity, but Austin flinched and was on his feet walking away without another word. Leyla leaned into Sally, who wrapped an arm around her shoulders.

Abe grunted again, which was almost the most commentary he'd contributed all night. He shook the dregs of his beer out onto the sand behind him and chucked his empty across to Noah, who tucked it in with the rest of the recycling. In the process, he wobbled into Mateo, who shored him up, rose, and gave him a hand up. Even if he'd been wearing his other arm, Abraham would be off-balance. He'd downed two beers for every one of Mateo's.

Leyla looked stricken, but Sally seemed to be reassuring her. He didn't doubt that Austin would reappear and clear the air between them with his defensive self-deprecation soon enough. Austin couldn't go ten minutes without circling round Leyla. But Mateo wasn't in the mood to wait for anyone to smooth things over. He wasn't in the mood to step back and consider anything, including whatever drove him to nudge at Abraham until he started walking. Once away from the light thrown by the fire, he spotted Austin perched on the café's patio rail, kicking back at it in a way that would leave his bare heels raw and angry. He steered Abraham that way.

Mateo waited until both brothers had their asses up on the railing, then planted himself in front of them. "You two are fucking this up."

Chapter Nineteen

She'd moved onto her balcony with a glass of wine and Prince playing in her earbuds. Not because she was trying to spy on the bonfire or anything. She didn't give one speck of consideration to what was happening at the bonfire.

Honestly, it was all a bit much for her at the moment. The Mateo stuff, sure, but also her sky-high stress levels and dirt-deep exhaustion. Being the one in charge of taking on board everybody's ideas and filtering them through the lens of her experience was frustrating and disheartening. Not always; sometimes she totally rocked it. But at the moment, she'd love for somebody else to come up with the perfect solution to their problem. Her ego wasn't bound up in being the brilliant one. Just in being the one who got the brilliance from idea to execution.

Her whole self was poised to sink into the crash-sizzle of the drum after the opening riff of *Purple Rain* when the raised voices of her brothers and her ex intruded past her earbuds.

If she could call him her ex. Hard to understand what to call him, since they hadn't been in an official relationship to start with.

Maybe her long familiarity with each of those voices made it easier for them to penetrate the bubble she'd been actively sinking herself into. She tucked the earbuds into her pocket and focused. It was a still night. The tide was low, so the waves were as distant as the laughter from her friends, or the pumps of rhythm emerging from her earbuds.

Still, it wasn't easy to eavesdrop. And maybe she'd have moved inside and slid shut the door, but she heard her name. And she'd heard Austin and Mateo curse. And she heard Abe's uncharacteristically raised voice. So, yeah, she was going to keep eavesdropping.

She moved to her balcony rail and looked down at the three of them. Her kitchen light was on, but the rest of her apartment was dark, so she didn't expect to call any attention to herself as she took in the tableau. Mateo, arms crossed and chin lifted as he glared at her brothers. Austin flailing until he knocked into Abraham, who swayed a little on the spot. At which point Austin wrapped his arm around their drunk big brother and hitched himself closer, but kept on talking.

"She said Surfside Swell was all about the town now. We had to accept our fate and hope Mrs. V keeps in mind why she and her husband chose to rent the bait shop to us in the first place."

"If that's her only focus now, why does she keep going back to banks?" Mateo asked.

"I don't know. Maybe she's just filling her time now that you've disappeared," her nosy asshole brother said.

Abraham reached to snag Mateo before he could turn away. "He doesn't mean that. No one blames you for calling it off. She's got her fixed ideas about doing things on her own, as if we're not a partnership. As if we didn't build Pier Three on collective principles."

Austin's leg was bouncing, which unbalanced him and Abraham both, but hell if she was going to call down to either of those judgmental gossips to warn them to be careful. Let them fall on their asses.

"I brought a solid idea to the table, but those two won't even consider it, much less bring it up at the all-staff meetings. So much for one person, one voice, one vote."

Abraham sounded exasperated. "It's not going to bring the cash we need in time for Mrs. V to not put the building on the market."

After that, maybe Mateo shuffled closer to her brothers, or maybe the wind shifted. Whatever it was, it got harder to make out the conversation. Abe said something about the right of first refusal, and Mateo mentioned the campaign again, which seemed to set Austin off on a tear about Leyla.

When he brought her up, all three men look towards the bonfire, and if Alicia wasn't so busy tending to her rage at her brothers, she might have spared a spark of sympathy for whatever Austin's latest stumbling block was with the studious surfer.

Mateo hadn't orchestrated leaving the bonfire with her brothers so she could overhear every word they exchanged. But he'd known she was up there, balcony doors open, when Austin posted up under her apartment.

He hadn't intended for her to have the chance to spy on their conversation, just like he hadn't intended to show up at the bonfire in order to be near her. They were where they were, though, so whether she liked it or not, he was going to have his say.

She'd told him once, long enough ago that he doubted she thought he remembered, that when they'd gotten the inheritance from their grandmother she'd been the one to propose the coffee shop and its founding principles of equity, sustainability, and asset-building for their employees who might not have had the advantage of generational wealth that the Wells family could bring to the enterprise.

He'd been blown away by the generosity and scope of her ambition. His gut had been fermenting unpleasantly since he'd learned of the roadblocks to her dreams. It was just fucking unfair that she wasn't getting to do the thing that meant so much to her, and to the world.

But as much as it stressed him to worry over Alicia, it pushed him dangerously close to the kind of permanent grudge he claimed to avoid, that her brothers would capitulate so easily to their business falling apart.

Not that they hadn't faced real obstacles. He got that, and respected that they faced them, too. But every way he looked at it, Alicia was the one making sure they had plans B, C, D, E, and F lined up, and was doing the pushing to ensure they gave as much of a shit about their corporate vision as she did.

"I get if you're burned out. I mean, everybody's burned out. It's been a hell of a few years, it'd be surprising if you hadn't faced that. But how can you two just decide to fail like this without being upfront with her about it?"

Abraham narrowed his eyes. "We're not making any decisions without her."

Mateo did glance up then, to see how much she was leaning down to catch their words. The problem was, she'd already caught him sticking his oar in, so unless he orchestrated the rest of their conversation where she could hear it all, he'd boxed himself into some craptastic choices.

He could keep talking behind her back about her brothers doing things behind her back, or keep his trap shut like he'd been minding his business all along. He was in a quandary of his own making.

That's what came of refusing to stay in one lane, as his father would be happy to remind him next time he mentioned having multiple career ambitions, or wanting to experiment with savory sweets, or being just as attracted to men as to women.

"Pick one thing and stick with it, Matt. Stay the course, Matt. Quit waffling, Matt."

Even if Papi's stroke-hampered speech was still unclear next time he brought it up, Mateo would know what he was saying.

He looked at the balcony again. This time, with a super obvious stare that Abraham and Austin couldn't miss. One by one, they turned to follow his gaze, before standing and following him out onto the pier.

"So she thinks we're making moves without her buy-in?" Austin demanded.

Mateo kept his pace up, not bothering to look at them. "I don't know what she thinks. I know what I think."

"And you think we're shafting her for our own convenience? You think we set out to destroy this thing we spent years building, with no thought to how it's going to affect her, or us, or any of the people we work with, or vendors we buy from, or the community we serve?"

Abraham added, "We're all committed to the business."

"Well, you've got a hell of a way of showing your unity," Mateo said, and if some of the bitterness in his voice was self-directed, that was fine. He was bitter.

Maybe he was more bitter that he couldn't charge in and solve Alicia's problems than he was that her brothers seemed to have abandoned her. Or maybe it was all bundled up with his sadness that she hadn't chosen to keep him around as sustenance or support. But her turning her back on him didn't make him any less inclined to help her, even as he felt the pain of her disregard.

He'd had to give up too many other choices in his life. He would hang on to his desire to make Alicia's life easier.

Abraham took ahold of his shoulder, pulling him to a stop. "Austin and I aren't hiding things from Alicia. Maybe it looks that way from the outside, maybe it feels that way to her. But that's not what we're doing."

They'd reached the intertidal zone. The waves lapping at the pier's posts and the creaking of weathered wood beneath their feet did nothing to lower his stress levels. He blew a breath out to sea. "It's not that I don't believe you. Or don't want to believe you. And you don't have to tell me to butt out, because I know I've got no right to speak on this. All that doesn't stop me from caring, though. Not just about Alicia, and never mind my own personal hell. I care about all of you, and everything Pier Three stands for, and what owning the building would make possible for you."

He did turn to them then, and found them exchanging heavy looks.

"I know I'm not full of news here. I didn't mean to explain your own career goals back at you. I just care. Even if it's not my place anymore to think about what Alicia has been through, even if it was never officially my place. I can't stop myself from wishing for her sake that she doesn't have to give up on Pier Three, and put herself back in on the job market."

Then Austin was at the edge of the pier, bouncing on his toes like he would throw himself into the ocean.

Abe drew in a sharp breath. "She told you what happened at Zenon?"

It was only his split-second parsing of the difference between surprise and curiosity that stopped Mateo from spilling her secrets. She'd blurted her truth in a move he'd— mistakenly, it seemed—taken as evidence of her opening her heart to his love. But he'd never suspected she'd been unlocking a vault she'd kept her brothers out of. "She never told you?"

Abraham shook his head once, and the full moon allowed him to see just how withdrawn and defensive the man was.

Austin was back in front of him. "What did she say?"

Mateo was silent, prompting Austin to throw his hands in the air and storm to the edge again. "She claims she never even thought of you as her partner, just her lover. But she can tell you, and not us?"

Mateo didn't hear what other infuriating and heartbreaking things he might have said, because he was too busy walking away.

Chapter Twenty

Suddenly her brothers couldn't leave her alone. She didn't know if they scheduled their hovering, or if they'd both tapped into the same overprotective instincts, but it was like she couldn't leave her apartment without encountering one or both of them.

The only reason she could breathe at all was that their parents were on vacation, which meant Abraham and Austin hadn't managed to alert them to whatever nonsense they'd internalized. Smallest of mercies, that she generally only encountered one excessively watchful member of her family at a time.

The three of them rarely had simultaneous shifts, preferring to stagger their hours behind the counter so one of them would be available if anything happened. But Austin puttered around doing side work every morning, even though that meant his skittering antics whenever Leyla showed up to meet a tutoring student, or just swung by for a drink after her morning on the waves. And Abraham kept stopping by to sit his grumpy ass down in the back corner, going over paperwork in the cafe instead of his usual habit of doing it in his apartment.

As soon as Alicia dealt with the last couple of customers in line, she marched over to her brother. "You two are being hella smothering. And I'm not here for it."

Abe glanced up like her laser eyes had never once put him in his place. "I'm just reconciling these invoices for you."

"Like hell you are. You're watching to see if I'm going to collapse into a puddle of feminine weakness."

He snorted. "I'd pay good money to see that."

"Oh, screw you. Why are you and Austin up in my face all the time now? What did Mateo say?"

"I thought you and Mateo were over. What's it matter what he says anymore?"

"It doesn't matter to me, to my heart or whatever." She sounded too aggrieved, and hustled on before her brother could call her on it. "I still want to know what he told you. Because you two have an acting like my babysitters since that night you bailed on bonfire."

"Pretty sure babysitters get paid."

"That is so not the point. He told you something."

"Are you admitting there's something to tell?"

"Oh, no you don't. You can't guilt me for choosing who gets to hear my secrets. My truth is mine, Abraham Augustus Wells."

He slipped off his ball cap and scratched his head. "Peace. I know it is. And, yeah, maybe, Austin and I have been stirred up about knowing there's something that you don't feel okay telling us. That's not ..." He shoved the cap back on and gestured to the chair across from him. "Sit down, okay?"

Her self-contained big brother was getting so suspiciously emotive that she decided to give him a chance, curious to see what emerged from this conversation. Even if she was still irritable with him.

She'd mustered a half-dozen rebuttals to his accusations about trust and transparency and brotherly love and section six of their partnership agreement by the time her ass hit the chair. Her parade of righteous thoughts crashed to a stumbling, synapse-destroying halt, though, when Abraham asked, "Why did you break up with Mateo?"

Alicia blinked. What non sequitur was her brother flinging at her now? "It's not like we were a real couple."

He crossed his arms over his chest, which was a pose he only pulled while wearing a prosthetic to make one of his super skeptical points. She snorted audibly enough for him to know that she hoped he'd bruised his chest with his terminal end.

"Nice."

"You're the one trying to derail me with random questions." And causing her less visible but still painful bruises by bringing up the subject.

"Yeah, so random, like: how is the guy you spend a bunch of your free time kissing not your boyfriend? Never mind free time. He's the guy you seek out in the middle of your work day."

"Not the middle."

"Okay, the beginning of your work day. Christ, I don't want to think about the specific times you had sex with the man."

"Fair enough. I don't want you to."

"The point is, you talk like it's just booty calls, but you act like it's your heart. He's the one you text nonsense with. He's the one you look for when you're in a crowd. And he's the one you share your secrets with. You spent all your time together. Now that you don't, you're sad."

Giving credence to his words seemed like a supremely bad idea, so Alicia settled for laser eyes. Even though it didn't seem to fool him one bit, maybe because her eyes were too damp to pull it off. The only one she seemed to be fooling was her own damn self, which, not unexpectedly, made her feel like a fool.

And Alicia was not in the mood to feel like a fool.

"What am I supposed to do? We broke up. He said he doesn't have room for me in his life. I'm supposed to start crying about how I was silly in love with him and never mind the fact that it's over now?"

Abraham scratched his beard, which was so not a helpful answer.

"Am I supposed to give up on everything I've ever set as a goal, just so I can throw myself at his feet and beg him to take me back? Am I supposed to accept his charging in unasked to save the day, just because I have trouble sleeping without him at night?"

Still no answers from her big brother, which only served to highlight how entirely she'd been hoping he would descend like some wise fairy and lay the perfect solution at her feet. Silly of her. That wasn't anything close to being in the wheelhouse of this particular careful, contemplative man.

Besides which, she could answer half her own questions by admitting that she only came up with them in self-defense against her whole entire chest cracking under the weight of her broken heart.

After a moment, Abraham stood with a shrug and walked off, leaving Alicia with so many more questions she didn't dare pose, for fear of what they'd reveal about her inner state.

Chapter Twenty-One

Jaxson and Quinn showed up at the bakery during the mid-morning lull. Eleanor flagged Mateo down and told him that it would be foolish to work himself into a state as unbalanced as his father's, and he should take the break she was offering, already. He grunted at her, which was not his most polite response, but she laughed as she pushed him to the customer side of the counter.

It was damn adorable how glowy Quinn had gotten since they'd hooked up with Jaxson. If he didn't like them so much, he'd succumb to jealousy. Not over Jaxson, cute as he admittedly was. But because of their overt happiness. "You're good?" Mateo asked.

"Yeah, and this pineapple empanada is my new favorite thing in the world, so thanks for being a brilliant baker. But listen, Jaxson, tell him," Quinn said.

"Tell me what?"

Jaxson fumbled a folder out of his backpack, and Mateo again considered cursing himself for not striking that very hot iron. But his heart wouldn't have been in it then, any more than it was now.

"So, look, my firm has been working on this revitalization measure, mostly the mixed use and affordable housing side of things. But I've been in some meetings, right?"

"Right." The city council had launched plan to help mitigate some of the socioeconomic impacts of the recession to its residents. Jaxson pulled out a map of the main commercial areas of Surfside. Everything from the beachside shops to the markets that bordered the residential areas in the foothills.

"So I was looking at the town map after bonfire the other night, and noticed a lot of those locally owned businesses your people were talking about. Also, some of the affordable and market rate housing sites, and that redevelopment of the transit hub—you know, where they're putting in more vehicle charging stations and the solar panels and bike shares?"

Mateo nodded, taking in the bird's eye view of Surfside. "You highlighted our shops."

"Mostly I grayed out everything that's not locally owned. The point is, look. Everything that's in color, I gave it a code. Green for the places already involved with Surfside Swell. Yellow for the ones you've asked but you haven't heard back from. Brown for the ones who said no."

"Not red?"

"I told him they didn't deserve a color from the rainbow," Quinn said.

Jaxson ducked his head a little, and Mateo went back to being charmed about how great they were together. Jaxson went on to explain his idea about turning the map into an interactive one on their website. And about using it to talk to the city council and other businesses. He turned back to Quinn. "Show him."

Quinn fetched their laptop out of Jaxson's bag and powered up. "You haven't changed the wifi password?"

"Marina won't let me," Mateo said.

They snickered. "That kid's a marketing genius, you know. I need to make her come work for me this summer."

Something in him twisted at the idea of spending all the summer days until his dad was out of rehab as the only James in the bakery. But he nodded. "I bet she'd love that."

Quinn pulled up a part of the Surfside Swell website he'd never seen. "It's a private page. Right now, only admins can see it. Point is, look." They clicked around a good bit, showing all the details he and Jaxson had been talking about. It worked as a town directory, putting everything into categories, highlighting. Something they called drilling down and cross-posting, with little embedded squares that linked to the websites of each of the businesses. It was all very fancy.

He whistled.

"Right?" Quinn nodded. "So what do you think? She'll like it, right?"

"Your girlfriend," Jaxson said. "Alice."

"Alicia," Quinn corrected.

"She's not my girlfriend."

Quinn huffed. "You're in love, whatever. You know I'm not hung up on labels."

Jaxson coughed an inside joke kind of laugh, and Mateo felt like he should slink back to the kitchen instead of being stuck in the middle of their intimacy.

Quinn blew a raspberry. "Hush. Answer the question."

"How can I if I'm hushed?" he asked, just to be a smartass. Also, he didn't like admitting how crushed his own mood was while sitting with these two and their endorphin highs. He sighed out his cowardice. "Alicia and I ended things, but, yeah, I know she's gonna love this. I'm no expert, but it looks like you two did something really brilliant here. Thank you."

Jaxson must have clocked how Quinn was struggling to react, so he jumped in with comments about wanting to help and believing in their mission and whatever kind of nonsense like that. "Also, that's not even the main thing."

He glanced at Quinn, who nodded encouragingly.

"I mean we're excited about the maps, but the main thing we wanted to suggest is ..." Jaxson licked his lips.

Quinn must have had their fill of waiting, because they blurted, "You should join the city council."

Mateo actually rubbed his ear to check his hearing. It wasn't necessary, but still. "I should do what?"

"Remember Noah was saying the one guy is retiring or quitting or whatever it is?"

"They call it resigning." Jaxson slid over the laptop and clicked on one of the other open tabs. "So we looked into it, and the council can appoint someone else to fill the rest of the term, which is like seventeen months. You meet all of the qualifications to serve. Residency and all that."

"But why me? There's got to be someone better." He gestured to the bakery like the self-explanatory albatross it was.

Quinn nudged Jaxson "See?"

Mateo glanced between them. "See what? What do you see?" He paced over to the bakery case pulled a few more empanadas out of it. "What can you possibly be seeing right now?"

He'd never thought anyone could bite into a pumpkin empanada smugly, but that's exactly what Quinn did. They swallowed and made a show of wiping their hands before saying anything else. "What he sees is that you're not asking, why would you want to? Or saying it's ridiculous. You just want to know why we think you're the right one."

"Well, that's ... I mean ..." Mateo felt flummoxed enough about his floundering to be happy when the door opened and his parents walked in.

"Papi, you're not supposed to be here."

His mom threw up exasperated hands. "This is what I told him. And what the doctors told him. But here we are."

Mateo shot an apologetic look at Quinn and Jaxson, who were packing away their stuff and crumpling up their napkins.

Quinn tapped their chest and mouthed, "Later."

Mateo hustled over to his dad. "If he's not supposed to be here, then why did you drive him here?"

"You can't blame me when I'm the one listening to him gripe all day," Mom said, pulling him down to kiss his cheek.

Papi grunted and muttered, Mateo thought, that he wasn't the one complaining.

And then he patted at Mateo's chest, which was as good as saying, "Calm down, Matt," which was all the icing he needed on this total burnt sheet cake of a day.

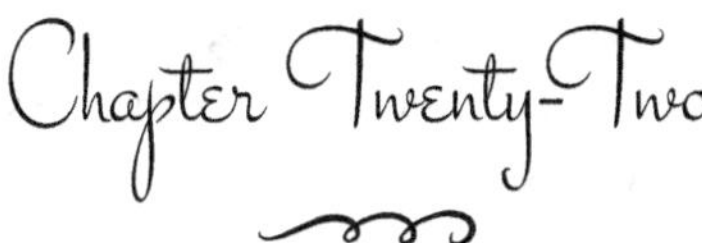

Alicia plucked at her guitar strings, the very definition of listless, but so what? If a woman couldn't get mournful while all by herself in her own apartment, what was even the point of feelings?

She should scramble herself an egg; she'd spent too many days in a row eating nothing but the stuff they sold downstairs. Tasty as that was, it left her a little short on some essential nutrients. So, fine. She planned out an entire spinach and mushroom omelet as she sat on her sofa, not bothering even a little bit to launch herself into the kitchen. Envisioning self-care ought to count for something, even if she never got around to doing the thing.

Her doorknob rattled, followed by the distinctive knock of Abraham's prosthetic on her door. Next up, the door rattled again. Austin called out, "Let us in."

Like they didn't know that if her door was locked, she wasn't in the mood. Of course, if she'd left it unlocked, she wouldn't be forced now to stand up and move across the apartment to greet them. "What."

"Hello to you, too." Austin pushed past her.

Abraham gave her a once over that made her squinch her eyes. "What are you doing?"

"I was about to get myself dinner," she said, and it wasn't like it was totally untrue.

He moved to her kitchen, pulling one of her filled water bottles out of the fridge. "Drink." He lifted his chin to Austin, who turned his random roaming intentional, gathering up the empty water bottles and other dishes she had scattered around. After Abraham scooted her to the dining table, he started pulling ingredients out of her fridge. Austin filled the sink with soapy water.

"What are you two up to?"

"Making dinner."

She glanced at the dark sky. "Haven't you already eaten?"

Abraham shrugged and Austin rummaged under her sink for a fresh sponge.

She didn't know why they thought they should come barging in and baby her like this.

Abraham got some rice going, whisked up a sauce, and set it aside before chopping up the half-wilted veggies she'd been totally saving for that omelet.

There was barely enough room in her little kitchen for the two of them. Far be it from her to jump into the middle of their unnecessary free labor. Austin wiped down her counters and carried the spray bottle of cleaner into the bathroom. He came out with her bathmat and hauled it and her entry mat onto the balcony, where he shook them vigorously and draped them, anchored under her flowerpots, over the railing.

All the while she considered the idea of moving back to her cozy spot on the couch. But it seemed like a lot of effort. And Abe was throwing some shrimp she'd forgotten was in her freezer into the stir fry. The problem with adulting only in her head was the tendency to overlook things like frozen seafood.

"Your cilantro has gone off," he said. It wasn't a question, so she maintained her silence. He shoved it, along with the vegetable scraps, into her compost bin. Austin, who was moving the first drying rack full of clean dishes back to her cabinets, handed Abraham a plate and grabbed a fork to fluff the rice.

Soon the cooking things were soaking in dishwater, four refilled water bottles were chilling in the fridge, and she was testing the heat level of the stir fry her brother set in front of her.

For as long as she could, she ignored them and ate. Eventually, she pushed back her nearly empty plate and rounded on her brothers. "You have to stop treating me like I'll shatter any minute."

"You're welcome," Abraham said, dry as anything.

She rolled her eyes his way. "Dinner was delicious. Thank you, Abraham."

He clearly didn't miss the goading petulance of her tone.

Austin plopped down across from her and interrupted whatever rebuttal Abe was planning. "So you know how I was talking to my friend about my production space idea?"

"Non sequitur much?" But apparently both of her brothers were done cutting her any slack.

"So Ty called me today, and two things. First is, a guy he knows who's moving overseas has some equipment to sell off. It's top line stuff—he was an independent producer, but he's taking a network job so he doesn't need his mics and mixers anymore. Plus, the different voltage. Or amperage? I don't remember. Something with electricity working differently."

Austin waved a hand like technical specifications were negligible, when every comparable business she'd looked at made elaborate meals out of their equipment details.

"But the bigger deal is, this family contact he has? Some friend of his parents, I guess, with a company that does ... I don't know, HR or something. Accountancy? Point is, no one wants to go into the office anymore. And there's enough key employees in the area that Ty said she's willing to sign a contract and pay some upfront costs to secure a place they can have weekly in-person meetings. With that setup, it's feasible for everyone to work remote the rest of the time."

Austin scanned every corner of her place, while she struggled with the intensity of how breezily he turned her personal space into a joint project. He wasn't shooting apologetic glances her way, or anything. His hands were clasped tight between jiggling knees. "I know it's probably not anything that'll give us the clout we need to afford the building. But most of what we'd need for setup can be transferrable to our new location, if our new landlord wants to knock this place down."

He shifted so his elbows were on his knees, leaning at her like his intensity made up for how he'd mentally boxed up all her paperbacks and houseplants.

"How much?" Abraham handed over another cold water bottle. "Ty's family friend. What kind of outlay is she talking about for us to get set up?"

Alicia slammed the water bottle down on her tiny dining table. It had taken her two weeks of thrifting and combing ads to find it, and it fit perfectly in the nook between her bar cart and her bookcase. And if her brothers had their way, she'd be dumping it on the curb ASAP. "Fine."

Austin scooted his chair so far back he nearly dislodged the to-be-read piles on top of her bookcase. "It's not a done deal, Alicia."

"No. Go for it. Nothing I did made the difference. I couldn't save the place, and we're out of time. Our only chance is to get this going and hope we can meet any offer once the building's on the market. Or hope for a landlord who ..." She waved her own hand, because they'd been over and over and over it all. Mrs. Vallejo had given her a deadline, and she didn't meet it.

"We."

She looked at Abraham, who'd moved to stand between them. "What?"

"We couldn't save the place. We all tried. It's not just you, and what happens next doesn't affect just you. If we end up having to move, that's on our partnership, not just on you."

Crossing her arms did nothing to contain the beating of her heart. "I'm the one who talked you two into a coffee shop."

"And I'm the one who couldn't get away from college fast enough, and Abe's the one who hates being around anyone except family and friends, and we're all the ones who busted ass to build the place and keep it going. It's a partnership, Lisha, and you act like it'd be your own personal failure if Mateo and Jaxson have to change the color-coding on the town map."

All her lined-up rebuttals fell down at that last statement. "Mateo and Jaxson what?"

"The map thing. On the website."

Austin's explanation explained nothing to her. She rubbed at the triceratops tattoo while she waited for more.

Abraham handed over her laptop, and a moment later she was exploring the Surfside Swell site. And learning that it wasn't 'Mateo and Jaxson' so much as 'Jaxson had an idea which he brought to Mateo and also they aren't sleeping together so stop flipping tables about that.'

"Plus, I guess he might have to recuse himself."

"No, it's only a conflict of interest if the bakery would profit directly," Abraham said.

At that, she had to ask for round two of explaining what was happening in Mateo's life. And then she had to ask for a minute to wrap her head around the idea of him sitting on the city council. Assuming they all pulled off the necessary back-ground shenanigans to put him there.

She palmed the cool water bottle and slinked back to her nest on the sofa.

Later. She'd process how disconnected they were, and how even so he was still doing things to help Pier Three, but later. First, she had to get graceful with her admission of defeat to her brothers.

Like he could tell he was welcome, Abraham sank into the seat beside her, lending his constancy and stillness to her turmoil. She drew in a breath, whooshed it out. "Okay. This is a blanket sorry and thank you, and if either if you need something more specific, I don't even know. Tell me, I guess."

Austin bark-laughed.

"And okay, also, I know it's a partnership. I asked for a partnership in the first place, remember?"

"Because Grandma would have approved."

She nodded at Abe. "Mostly of the part about using the money to make lots of lives better, not just ours. But, yeah. Okay. I've been acting like I'm the only one with stakes here, and that's crappy of me. I know it matters to all of us, and I appreciate how much you've both worked towards a solution. Even if it means I'm sleeping on your sofa from now on."

"I'm sure Mom and Dad would let you go back to your room at their place." Austin grinned like the evil brat he was.

"Yeah, no. What part of 'being an independent adult answerable to no-one' did you misunderstand?"

"What part of 'you can be your own boss but still accept help from your family and partners' did you misunderstand?"

Abraham wrapped his arm around her and squeezed her shoulder. "The kid's not wrong."

"Shut it." She rubbed circles at her temples and sighed. "Fine. Let's see if Austin's plan saves the day. Or at least gives us a cushion for when we incur moving and refitting expenses. When do you need me out?"

All the logistics should have given her a bit of energy. She always did prefer a plan to aimlessness. But no matter how they coordinated and strategized, Alicia never stopped feeling like her heart was dragging a half-step behind everything else whirring around her.

Chapter Twenty-Three

Alicia double checked her bag and the tray of drinks, like there was some possibility that catastrophe had befallen them on the short drive between Pier Three and the James house. Foolish, procrastinating nonsense. So, she knocked.

Ms. James ushered her in with her usual wreathed in smiles thing, but with a new, haggard undertone. "Mateo's not here, sweetie. He's at the bakery."

"No, I guessed. I just wanted to drop this off. It's the smoothie Marina likes, and these two are different, high protein ones, no sugar. One's spinach and ginger, and this one is berries and mango. I thought they might be a nice supplement to Mr. James's diet. There's a paper in the bag with the information so you can run it past his nutritionist if you need to." She was over-talking, and way too aware of it.

"Oh, sweetie. You're too good to us."

She tried to shrug off the praise, but Ms. James was having none of it. And then she really wielded the emotional sledge-hammer at Alicia. "Our Mateo is a lucky boy. I know Greg would say it anyway, because of your gender, but that's not why I say so. I feel blessed to see him happy with someone as thoughtful and giving as he is."

Really the last thing that either one of them needed was for her to start crying, but that's where they were.

"Pobrecita. Come here." And next thing she knew she was getting hugged by this woman whose strong arms and flour-soft shirt were such echos of Mateo.

"Sorry. I'm sorry, Ms. James. I just, that was really sweet of you to say. I don't think of myself that way but ... knowing him." She rubbed under her eyes. "It's such a cliche, but I learned so much about it, about being giving, from your son. I've spent a lot of years now feeling like the most important thing was for me to look out for myself, and ..." She sniffed and shrugged.

"Well, that is important, of course."

She nodded. "I know. But all that tension all that time, feeling like it was me versus everything else, put me in a defensive kind of headspace. And I think—no, I know—Mateo is the one who coaxed me out of it."

"Well, sweetie, that's what we want out of love, right? To bring out the best of each other, like me and my Greg." The woman was relentless with that sledgehammer of hers.

She fought the urge to clutch her chest like her torso was ready to spill all of her guts. "Sorry for being so emotional, Ms. James."

"Call me Marie."

"Sorry for being so emotional, Marie. I just—I wanted to drop off these drinks. And there's a few books in here, light reading. I thought to help distract you some while you're waiting at rehab for Mr. James."

"Greg."

"Okay, for Greg." She smiled, and aimed to leapfrog past all her oversharing emotion by asking about rehab.

Marie gave her a rundown, brushing back a few tears of

her own. "It's a lot, I'm not gonna lie. But our Mateo has been so good, stepping up at the bakery. Once he gets this notion about city council out of his head we'll all be so pleased."

She must have given a lot away with her face before she schooled herself, because Marie questioned her in a way that would have felt way too personal if she hadn't just gone through several of the woman's tissues. "Well, we just don't know how long Greg will be out. Doesn't this seem like too much to take on right now? If he waited until the next election, maybe."

"If he waits until the next election, he'll have to go through more rigmarole to get on the ballot. Plus, campaigning would eat up a lot more time than being appointed for now will. To me, it seems if he wants to do it, he should get support from his family. You just got done telling me how selfless and giving he is. Which is exactly how you raised him. It's the reason he's given up so much to work at the bakery, even though that's not his ideal job."

Marie straightened slowly. "What do you mean the bakery isn't his ideal job?"

She was sure Mateo had said this to them over and over. He had griped about their reaction more than once. No matter how much this wasn't her place to say, she and Marie had crossed a dozen lines in the ten minutes she'd been there. So she laid it out as clearly as she understood it. "He works for you because you ask it of him, and he respects what you and Greg have built. And his grandparents before that. He's said this to you before."

Marie plucked at her shirtsleeve. "Mateo never—well, when he was young, but ..."

They grimaced at each other.

"I'm sure I'm overstating the case," Alicia said, though she wasn't. What was she supposed to do? Tell this lovely woman that her bisexual son had made a bargain with his ailing father to rein in his homophobia as long as he otherwise did what was expected of him?

Back when they were first together, she'd worried that his feelings for her were caught up in knowing that being with a woman kept his father's comments at bay. Mateo said that wasn't it, and she was in no position to question his truth or his love.

Except she really hadn't done much in the way of making herself easy for him to love, had she? So never mind that theory.

She made nice and wished Greg well and got the hell out of Mateo's family home.

Noah pulled Mateo aside as soon as he got to bonfire, launching into a thousand details about Surf Fest and the city council. The guy had done a ton of homework. Impressed, Mateo dragged him over to confer with Jaxson and Quinn. They were huddled in a group talking strategy and next steps when Mateo's nerves went silly alert.

He threw a glance over his shoulder. Alicia was approaching, and his legs had him halfway to her before he noticed he was walking away from a legit important conversation. He paused for a second to check on the others. Noah was shaking his head, but waved him off. Nothing like a group of friends too wrapped up in his business to let him hide anything. At least he didn't have to explain to them why he was beelining to Alicia like his heart depended on it.

Which it did.

He should have expected how tentative her smile would be, but seeing it wobble sent a pang through him. He wanted to wrap her up and wipe away all of her nervousness, but things needed saying.

"You're here," she said. The joy in her tone ignited in his chest like the sizzle of the bonfire behind him. "I wasn't sure. I was afraid you'd be too wiped out, with everything at the bakery and stuff. Your dad and—"

"And city council?" he asked.

Her lips pressed together. "I need to say this. I interfered with your family, talked out of turn, and I'm really sorry."

At that, he gave up to fight to stay self-contained, and grabbed her hands. "Do not apologize for that. I love that you did it. I love that you talked to Mom, and I love how much a difference a made for me."

"Yeah?"

He nodded. "Yeah. It—it made me feel special." His face burned hot, and he wasn't nearly close enough to the fire to blame anything but how he still felt soft and tender at the idea of Alicia going to battle for him like that.

"You are special."

Maybe he pulled away some at that, because she squeezed his hands and stepped closer.

"Mateo. You're the most special."

He fully collapsed into her then, dragging their bodies flush and dropping his head to hers. Her hair smelled of coffee and the sea, and her warmth radiated so perfectly into him. His whole self thrummed with rightness.

Her hands on him were restless. "You said you need space, and I didn't go to your parents' house to take that away from you. Your mom accused me of being thoughtful, and I hope I was."

"You were." He wanted to stop her fretful spill of words, but he also wanted to hear every syllable she had in her.

"If I was, though. That's what I was trying to explain to her, when I went and intruded on your family dynamics—if I was thoughtful, it was because you make me thoughtful. Your whole life is about finding ways to do good things, and I admire it so much. You know that, right? Because you give me so much grace, Mateo."

Her eyes, and the press of her fingers on him. The way her hair rippled in the breeze like the waves behind her. Every word she said, and the way she stood in her truth to say them.

She'd stolen his voice, so all he could do was whisper, "A."

Chapter Twenty-Four

She gasped and tried to burrow deeper into his hold, like doing so would stop the tears. He was the one who caused them to fall in the first place.

He squeezed her right back, muttering something beyond her ability to understand, and never letting up the pressure that she so needed. She was dimly aware of her brothers and friends chattering around the bonfire, but the only thing she could focus on was finding out if this was a more tearful good-bye, or the chance to start anew.

"Do you need to go back and talk to everyone about your council seat?"

"I like how you take for granted that I'm going to get the appointment." The smile in his voice buoyed her.

"Of course you're going to get the appointment. With this crew behind you and everything you already do for the community? I'm surprised they didn't cold call you to join already. You're bound to be on some kind of Good Citizen watch list."

"Well, that sounds ominous."

"If it turns out be true, don't let me know. I doubt it's safe for civilians like me to be clued in to this kind of thing." Just when she thought his hold on her was at its peak, he tightened it and swung them in a circle. She drummed on his shoulders, but she didn't mean it. As far as she was concerned, he could take up the permanent position of her personal transport mechanism.

Someone at the bonfire wolf-whistled at them. The only one she could rule out was Abraham, who didn't know how to whistle, much to the ongoing amusement of her and Austin.

They laughed and Alicia leaned back to look at him. "Do you want to go back to the bonfire, or?"

Mateo was already shaking his head. "I can catch up with all them later. I think they already plan to come by the bakery tomorrow."

"I don't want to—" She cleared her throat, because she *did* want to, but she was trying to be respectful of his space. "If you have the time, I'd love for you to come up to the apartment."

He was setting off that way without having fully put her down. She wriggled a little until her feet touched the sand again. A chorus of goodnights came from the group around the bonfire. She waved her hand over her head without bothering to respond or to go back for the serape she'd dropped when he first approached her. Her cousin or her brothers or someone would see to it, and if not, well, that would be one less thing to pack.

She stopped before they got to the stairs. "So, I don't want to throw you for a loop when we get up there."

"Oh?"

She nodded. "Thing is—okay. Come on up and I'll explain it." Because she wanted to be where he could read her expression in the full light. Wanted to give him the chance to make decisions without the pressure of an audience, or the uncertainty of conversations held in darkness.

Small as her beloved studio apartment was, the moment she'd begun boxing it up, it felt like she owned a robber baron's worth of material goods.

"You're moving?"

Alicia took his hand and navigated past cartons so they could sit. "It seems like Austin's plan might work. And even if it doesn't, it'll give us a cushion towards whatever's next."

"So that means, what?"

She didn't want to stay on her side of the sofa. But: he'd asked for space. Even if he was throwing his hat in the city council ring, and finding time to enjoy bonfire nights, and consulting on ways to make the Surfside Swell campaign stronger, she didn't officially know that he wanted to open himself to a relationship with her.

She laced her fingers around the knee she'd tucked up to her torso. "It means I'm moving, yeah. Not sure where yet. Mom and Dad have units available, but I don't know that I want to be that surrounded by family. I maybe had to accept that I'm in a partnership with Abe and Austin, but that doesn't mean I want to live under the same roof as them."

"Move in with me."

"Mateo."

"A."

His dear, sincere face. His bright eyes and strong shoulders. "I love that you offered. And ... maybe yes, but not just now. I've been so lonely up here without you, Mateo. I hope you believe that. Not just that you've gotten me so addicted to your touch. It's so much more than missing the sex."

He groaned a little, shifting in his seat, and she had to bite her lip.

"I know. Trust me, I know. Thing is, we've been lovers for so long now."

"Been too long."

She knew he meant since they last slept together, not that their relationship was overlong. The tension rippling across his body spurred her to blurt out all her hopes and plans. "Thing is, too, that I know what we're like as lovers. And as friends. And ... well, no complaints there."

He huffed his agreement.

Alicia fiddled with the capo she'd rediscovered when packing up her desk drawers. "Right. But what we haven't done, not properly, is explored what we're like as a couple. Which I know is all to do with me and the brakes I've always put on us."

Mateo slumped back. "This is all sounding like another set of brakes. I love you, A, but if you need us to go back to where we were, I don't know how easily I could take that."

He was so damn noble, professing his love while simultaneously giving her permission to define what she needed. Even if it hurt him. She couldn't hold to her side of the sofa any longer. In one quick lunge, she straddled him and wrapped her arms around his back.

His head came up, and his hands bracketed her hips. "Hi."

"You love me?"

He licked his lips.

"Or should I put that in the form of a statement? You love me."

Mateo eyed her for a long moment, and finally grinned. "Fine, yes. I love you. And I've explored plenty what being part of a couple with you is about."

She grinned right back. "Cool. That's half the battle, then."

"We're in a battle still?"

They'd been tilting together, and their foreheads came to rest against each other. "All the signs point to us winning the war, if that helps. What I think is, we're going to settle real fast into being goofy in love, and living together, and making a life together."

His hands spasmed, pinching her pelvis with delicious pressure.

She closed her eyes to remember all she had to say without falling into his eagerness. "But what I don't want is for all this lust between us, and the fact that I have to move, to push us into something before we know we're ready for it. Maybe it's silly, but I want to be smart about how I go about falling desperately in love with you."

"A. Why are you taunting me?"

She wanted to say it back, his words of love, but also, she didn't. They needed—she needed—time to settle into their commitment. Time to settle into the comfort of being a couple, to reframe their time together in deeper and wider ways than just their physical connection. To assure herself that she wasn't leaping at him out of fear. "I'm trying to not be scared about this. Make sure I'm committing because I'm as sure as the tides, not because I'm, I don't know, lonely and bummed that I wasn't the one to save the coffee shop. If it's even saved like we hope. That's been the one thing I've been trying to accomplish for so long now—since we opened, in a lot of ways. And I failed."

"Hey."

"Okay, not failed in the most doomed sense." She forced herself to remember all those years of paying a living wage and building sustainable pathways to collective leadership. "For a long time—too long, I know—I told myself I had to be in charge so I didn't make myself, make any of us, vulnerable to a toxic workplace again. And that blocked me from telling myself the real truth: that making myself invulnerable meant I was locking myself away not just from the bad, but from so much good."

"Fuck, you're amazing." He'd gone all man-of-few-words

on her again, but his face shared all his secrets. The loudest of them was his love for her, and she felt so grounded and alive and willing to throw herself into whatever he could dream up next.

A plan. She'd invented a plan. Something to do with solidity and knowing herself and approaching life in a series of loving partnerships.

So instead of launching into an unconsidered happily ever after, she whispered her promises in the kiss she gave him. Promises about respecting and trusting him, about keeping her heart open for him, about joy. He gave them right back to her, his kiss a covenant she was happy to sign.

Drawing back, she met his half-smile with a full one of her own. "I do have something you can help me with, though."

"Okay."

She laughed. "You don't have to agree before I even ask. You're always doing that. You need to protect your time better."

It was fun to feel Mateo's muscles bunch and move when he shrugged. "You're my A. I'm going to give you all the time I can."

"Impossible man." She kissed his cheek. Then his other cheek. "Fine. I'll take some help apartment hunting. I've got some listings picked out, and I'd normally ask Austin to check them out with me, but he's thrown himself head-first into this studio conversion. You're the second-most handy person I know, so I thought you'd be good for spotting any pitfalls."

"I'm just going to pick the one closest to my place."

She fell against his arm, giggling. "Can we have sex now?"

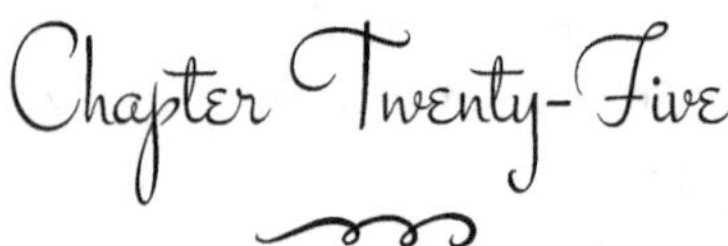

Chapter Twenty-Five

Alicia knew Mateo loved her. She planned to make them a priority. She stood up to his family for him.

He could work with it.

"Yes." He meant to the sex, but also: to everything. To her cautious but hopeful plans. To courtship. To a future side by side.

To any small quests like apartment hunting or to big ones like making Surfside a more equitable place for people who'd lived too long with systemic barriers.

And to the sex. He surged to his feet, carrying her with him, bypassing packing boxes to get to bed. Her laughter and the way her legs cinched his waist and every coffee and salt and citrus scent of her.

Too long apart. Too many worries: about his dad's health; about how to navigate the demands of the bakery with neither parent available to work; about exploring every avenue in his goal to secure the council seat. About the fragile state of his heart.

All of it swept to the side like the pillows and blankets on her bed before they tumbled to it. Their hands were all frantic motion to strip each other, to stroke every expanse of skin they uncovered. Their lips never let up. Kisses, nips, loving words. The bite she left over his heart. He moaned. "Alicia. God."

"Seriously." She grinned up at him and his pulse was a damn problem. It was racing faster than could be healthy. If he had any spare brain cells to devote to worry, he'd add it to the list.

But no. The only thing he could do was relish every second he was touching her. Soak up every sound. And savor every taste. He slid down her body, using his torso to wedge her legs wider for him. She sent her hands drifting after him, tangling with his at her nipple, tickling his nape as she reached for a hold in his hair. He worshiped her navel, breathed a thanksgiving prayer over her jutting hips. And finally—too long, far too long—ran his thumbs through the curls on her labia, parting her and revealing the swollen nub of her clit.

It might have been far too long, but he was incapable of forgetting the exact pressure she liked, the strumming touch and the agonizing-to-them-both wait for his lips to close on her. The yank at his hair, the thrust of her pelvis. The way her encouragement got breathier and breathier before she sank into a keening hum and incoherence.

Fuck but she tasted good.

He couldn't help but to thrust against the bed some when she came in his mouth. It was all too glorious and too precious and too erotic and too fun.

"Mateo, damn." She tugged on his hair again, this time a gentle command to move to her side. He was more than happy to obey because the satisfaction of satisfying her hadn't taken much of the edge off at all. He needed to kiss her. Needed her to taste herself on his lips. Needed.

"My Mateo."

Needed, it turned out, the devotion in her voice. The tender gleam in her dark eyes. "I love you, A."

She didn't say it back, but her smile grew wider and more welcoming. Like she was prepared to take his love, instead of fighting it. Like she didn't have any questions about the rest of their lives.

Her lamp was on but that didn't explain his glow. Mateo absolutely radiated emotion at her, and it felt like a balm and a blessing.

Also, super sexy. The orgasm: top-notch. But she wasn't about fighting the restless need for him to fill her. She wanted his thrusts, damnit.

So she pulled herself over him. Gave his cock a few strokes, unbearably content to once again hold his girth.

"Killing me, woman."

"Fair play." She kept swallowing giggles, then reminding herself she was allowed to be as silly-happy as she wanted. The reminder only made her more sober, though. More intent to show him how serious she was about those unstated promises she'd made.

So before sinking onto his length, she leaned in for another kiss. It wasn't shockingly different from any other kiss they'd shared. The firm press of their mouths together, their gentle exploring tongues. The quirk of his lips and the huff of her breath.

But somehow, it was more. It was a pact, and a capitulation. A tumbling into—and an embrace of—inevitability.

"Mateo." She guided his cock, lowered until he filled her core. Stilled and cupped his cheek. "I love you."

"Oh, fuck." He gripped her ass and her back, flipped them. Drove into her and into her. "A. I love you. But."

His thrusts didn't let up. Her clit was thrumming, and she spared a hand to help it along.

"You don't have to say it. You're not ready. I don't care. I can wait."

He was altogether too coherent, so she wrapped her legs up around his ribcage and dug her spare hand into his shoulder for leverage. "Wait all you want. I'm going to come again."

Then she lost her words for a few minutes. And, to her immense pleasure, so did he. Moans and grunts and her high cries while he slid his length in and out of her, relentless, perfect. All-consuming. She shattered into another intense orgasm, her heels pounding happily on his back. Mateo's kisses went sloppy, sliding from her cheek to her neck to her ear.

She pushed him to his knees and arched up to meet him, planting his palms on her breasts. He obliged, cause he was Mateo, and his favorite thing was to please her.

Turned out, her favorite thing was to please him in return.

As his pace increased, she caught his hand and squeezed it. "Don't want you to wait."

He threw his head back in a glorious groan, half-lifting her into his lap as he emptied into her. Never letting go of her hand. It surprised another orgasm out of her, and there she went, laughing again. And they curled on the mattress facing each other, hands linked, smiling eyes and entangled feet and just a ridiculous amount of happy flowing between them.

When her breath was caught, her thumb traced circles on the back of his hand. "I still mean it. About us being careful to build our relationship up on solid foundations."

His lips flattened some, but after a slow blink his eyes were still tender. "I know. It's a good plan. I'm on board."

This man was just too self-sacrificing. Good thing she was sticking around to look out for him. "Glad to know it. But you know you can tell me when you disagree, and we'll work something out, right? You don't have to be the only one giving stuff up all the time. It's not 'Alicia gets everything, even if Mateo gets nothing.' That's not how I want to treat the guy I love."

His tears surprised her. But so did her own.

"A." One tiny syllable, full of tenderness, acceptance, hope, and a future built by working problems out together.

In other words, everything.

Epilogue

All that apartment hunting, and she still ended up living in her parents' building, two doors down from her brothers. At least they didn't share a common wall. She didn't need their comments about her nightlife.

Even after moving, she kept the opening shift at Pier Three, which helped all three of them maintain their balance. If she slept at Mateo's, she'd maybe swing by her place in the early hours after he rose for baking. If he stayed at hers, she got a bit of extra sleep once he'd pulled her blanket over her and kissed her goodbye.

Other nights they didn't spend together. Sometimes for self-imposed   building-their-relationship-carefully   reasons. And sometimes for logistics. There was the night he was out late at a council meeting, and drinks afterwards with the community policy group. Though his dad wasn't back in the kitchen, he was well enough for both the James parents to take the morning shift once in a while.

That was one of the first things his dad made clear, when Mateo was appointed to fill out the council term: one of his therapy goals was to recover enough to give Mateo time to pursue his community service.

It meant everything to him, so Alicia was pretty happy about it, too.

Six-thirty in the morning, and as soon as she set the grinder to work on the day's first batch of beans, she stepped outside to watch Mateo pull the bakery van into the little space beside what used to be her stairs. The scent of the medium roast followed her, hitting the wall of sea air outside and filling her with comfort and a sense of rightness.

"A." He moved to her instead of heading to unload the delivery.

"Hey, morning. How'd it all go last night?"

"Good. The Fair Wage initiative is underway, so Quinn should be able to add the signers to the website when they get a chance."

"Awesome. I'm glad it worked out."

"I missed you in my bed, though."

She squeezed his hands. "About that."

Mateo's eyes crinkled. He wrapped his arms around her in one of his glorious, encompassing hugs. "That sounds promising."

"Well, mostly. You remember my friend Callie?"

"She's the artist?"

"Yeah." She bit her lip. "The not-promising part is, she had a fire. She lost all kinds of stuff—clothes, paperwork. Just about everything, really. But the worst of it is, she had a bunch of pieces ready for a show. And they're almost all gone now. Plus, insurance has her set up in some grim studio hotel. It's a real mess. Anyway, I told her to come up here and stay at my place."

"Your ... one bedroom place?" He squeezed her to him, because he was sharp, and could guess where she was going.

"Yes, well. That's the promising part. I think it's time."

She meant to go on. To explain about subletting to Callie, and tease him about how he'd already stocked his shower with her favorite products, and explain the brilliant plan she had for how to rearrange his bedroom to fit her armoire. But instead, he was kissing her, and that meant she didn't need to go on. Didn't need to ask if he was okay with the idea. Didn't need to say she wouldn't move in if he wasn't ready for her.

Because Mateo was pressing her up against the door of the van, and kissing her, and she was surrounded by the fruit-nut-coffee scent of the cafe, and the yeasty aroma of the bakery, and the salt tang from the Pacific.

And Mateo, who encompassed and surpassed it all.

Thank You!

This first book of my new Pier Three Coffee series is dear to my heart. I'm so excited to introduce you to my fictional world of Surfside, CA, and to the Wells siblings.

I went to college in Santa Cruz, CA, and my sons both attended California colleges and live in the Bay Area, so the town of Surfside draws heavily on places where I've spent many bright and busy months of my own life.

The Pier Three Coffee trilogy is going to be quite the adventure for the Wells siblings, all of whom are super people but with ... let's call them quirks. They'll figure it out in their own ways, with the help (and sometimes hindrance) of their romantic co-leads.

Eager to find out if Austin can be *the one* for Leyla? So is he! Unfortunately, you and he have to wait until **Latte for Leyla**, while Austin watches another sibling get what he most wants in **Cappuccino for Callie**

Thanks for reading!

-Melanie

Acknowledgments

The big joy of writing fiction—of writing romance, in particular—is the chance to create a world readers want to enter no matter what's up in their real lives.

Developing Surfside and the world that Alicia and Mateo inhabit brought me such happiness. And I couldn't have done it without the support and advice of so many people.

My family, of course. I know authors often list their family last in their acknowledgments, because there's no easy way even for wordsmiths to express their incalculable gratitude for the cheerleading, ear-lending, dishes-washing, and so on. But in the past couple of years, my family has learned to live and work in constant proximity to each other, so my husband and sons got front row seats to the often nonsense ways I go about filling my days as an author. And they made room for me even while they were (let's be grumpy here) intruding on what I'd come to expect was a solitary work life. Love you tall men, and thanks for filling my days with music and tortilla chips.

I grew up with parents who owned and worked for the business my grandfather founded, and I, too, worked in that business for most of my adult life. I learned so much more than my love of spreadsheets from my time at FII, and I hope all the truly great parts about working for my parents, and working with my sister when we became co-executives, translates to what you've read about James Family Bakers and Pier 3 Coffee.

As always, I'm grateful to Robert for the editing, and to

Rae for hers, and to my online writing community, especially my fellow CRW board members and my #notwriting and IRP peers. Cheers to you all!

About the Author

Melanie Greene lives in a tiny woodland cottage in a big skyscraper city, with her husband and kids and cat and dog and all the people inhabiting her imagination.

For more info, visit her at www.melaniegreene.com, where you can sign up for her newsletter to access new releases and bonus content. Also visit her at Facebook.com/MelGreeneBooks and Twitter.com/Daki_MelGreene.

9 781941 967287